Training School for School for Negro Girls

Camille Acker

 **FEMINIST PRESS**
AT THE CITY UNIVERSITY OF NEW YORK
NEW YORK CITY

Published in 2018 by the Feminist Press
at the City University of New York
The Graduate Center
365 Fifth Avenue, Suite 5406
New York, NY 10016

feministpress.org

First Feminist Press edition 2018

 This book was made possible thanks to a grant from the New York State Council on the Arts with the support of Governor Andrew M. Cuomo and the New York State Legislature.

 This book is supported in part by an award from the National Endowment for the Arts.

First printing October 2018

Cover and text design by Suki Boynton

Library of Congress Cataloging-in-Publication Data
Names: Acker, Camille, 1978- author.
Title: Training school for Negro girls / Camille Acker.
Description: New York : Feminist Press at the City University of New York, 2018.
Identifiers: LCCN 2018011235 (print) | LCCN 2018016435 (ebook) | ISBN 9781936932382 (ebook) | ISBN 9781936932375 (trade pbk.)
Classification: LCC PS3601.C535 (ebook) | LCC PS3601.C535 A6 2018 (print) | DDC 813/.6--dc23
LC record available at https://lccn.loc.gov/2018011235

"An exciting literary achievement by a significant emerging talent. This flawlessly executed work reinvigorates the short fiction genre."　　　　　　　**—BUST**

"A timely, welcome book."　　　　　**—THE MILLIONS**

"Acker shows that the lives of black girls and women are vast and varied, pushing back on the monolithic ways they are often portrayed."　　　**—KIRKUS REVIEWS**

"These stories pulse with vitality as ordinary people look for a future in a world that doesn't expect them to have one."　　　　　　**—FOREWORD REVIEWS**

"Camille Acker navigates her characters' lives with humor, heart, and grace. I love these stories."

—LISA KO, author of *The Leavers*

"These are stories that bring to mind the life lessons of classic R&B tunes: *It ain't right, but it's okay*; *If loving you is wrong, I don't want to be right*; *How sweet it is to be loved by you*. Training School for Negro Girls is a symphony of story: the clear, true voices of girls and women who are shaping who they might be against the constraints of the weights and counterweights of race and history and gender. A marvelous book."

—VERONICA CHAMBERS, author of *Mama's Girl*

"*Training School for Negro Girls* is a vivid, engaging book. Camille Acker takes a giant leap into the American literary scene as a necessary new voice."

—ROBERT BOSWELL, author of *Tumbledown*

"Acker's compelling stories vibrate with fresh portrayals, vivid prose, and real attitude. In her hands, we see Washington, DC, anew, as a backdrop for black girls coming into their own. *Training School for Negro Girls* is both a rich compilation of storytelling and a deft guide for living; as you witness these characters learn their heartbreaking lessons, you too might never be the same."

—BRIDGETT M. DAVIS, author of
*The World According to Fannie Davis:
My Mother's Life in the Detroit Numbers*

"A devastating and subtle portrayal of what it is to be black and female in America: the ache, the rage, the sorrow, the unending will to rise."

—SHOBHA RAO, author of *Girls Burn Brighter*

"*Training School for Negro Girls* stands as a wise testament to possibility, laying out the means by which we can all weather the worst circumstances and survive the most perilous times. A stunning achievement."

—JEFFERY RENARD ALLEN, author of
Song of the Shank

"Acker has written pages that are saturated with the stuff of black life in Washington, DC: the cadences, the music, the aspirations, the trouble, the disappointments, the inventiveness, and the laughter. *Training School for Negro Girls* is a wonderful debut."

—JAMEL BRINKLEY, author of *A Lucky Man: Stories*

To all the black women close to my heart and to
the two who are closest, Fay Acker and Juliette Acker.

CONTENTS

We are looking for girls of the finest character. This is a select school. There is such a great need for young women of talent and leadership ability, who really want to let their lights shine in this "confused" world . . .

—NANNIE HELEN BURROUGHS,
Founder, National Training School
for Women and Girls, Washington, DC

PART ONE

The Lower School

WHO WE ARE

We walk down the halls like we are coming to beat you up. Even the teachers move out of the way. No one wants to catch an elbow in their ribs or a foot in their stride. They look away when we pass. Or take a turn down a hallway where we are not. We will make them into a joke anyway. Something about their face. Or their clothes. Or their name. We decide who they are.

When we go to lunch, we take up three tables. We need only two. Nobody will ask us to move. We sign up for the same classes. The easy ones. The white kids want the advanced placement classes. They make you take tests to get into them. Tests we never have liked. We don't like teachers either. They tell us what to do. We don't let anybody tell us what to do.

We cut class. Almost every day. The security guards are black like us so we just dap them up. Then, we go. When we leave, we go to the movies down the street. Pay for one. And then go theater to theater seeing all the shows we want.

We eat. At McDonald's. Or the Chinese takeout. Or sometimes we go to nicer places where they give you real menus. We sit there eating and laughing. The owners say we should quiet down. We decide that to teach them, we won't pay. And we run out on the bill. Sometimes even when they don't say something, we run out on the bill.

And then we stroll all around Upper Northwest. We walk past real nice houses with real nice cars. Only one car in the driveway. The other one gone. Probably in some garage at the State Department. Or on the Hill. Or Downtown at one of the law firms. Every house has a big porch and around Christmas they have lights wound around the columns. A lit-up plastic snowman. A wreath on the door. And at Halloween, the houses have a skeleton and cotton made to look like cobwebs. A cackling witch.

We go to school with some of their kids. Or their kids go to Sidwell. Or Holton-Arms. Or Georgetown Day. Their kids take classes at colleges too. A couple of days a week at American or GW. They come home and tell their parents about how the Germans get talked about more for what they did in World War II, but some people think the Japanese were worse. We don't tell our parents things like that. We pretend we don't even know things like that.

We go to this field with this old, abandoned stage. We sit there because we don't sit in grass like white people. We sit on the warped old wood. It cracks and we crack on each other. And sometimes we make out. And sometimes we act like having someone else's tongue in our mouth is nice. Or that having hands on our body is good. When we get to underwear, we stop there so we don't get embarrassed.

And some days there is alcohol from a cousin who says not to tell our parents, and some days there is alcohol from way back in the cabinet on the lower right side of our parents' stash. Once or twice, there is weed. And we lie on the stage, venturing splinters, surrounded by each other, not looking anybody in the face. And we feel lots of things we can't say. Until we hit each other or pull each other's hair and go back to pretending we don't feel anything at all.

When we leave for the day, we get on the Metro. We swing around the poles. And lean over the people sitting in priority seating and act like we're looking at the map. We laugh and curse and scream. The people in suits and ties and nice dresses and heels give us looks. Until. They turn to look out the window. Or look down into their *Washington Posts*. We talk louder to make them look. And we don't stop until we see that they're afraid. That they walk way down to the other end of the subway car to exit through that door instead of the door near us.

We always see an old lady on the train. Not the same one, but one tough enough to not look away. We won't notice at first that she sees us. Then, when we do, we call her out on it.

"Excuse me, ma'am?" we say. "I'm sorry to bother you, ma'am."

"Yes?" she answers and smiles.

"Well, ma'am, I wanted to ask you a question. If it's not too much trouble," we say with our serious face.

"Go ahead," she says. Encouraging us. Discouraging her fears.

We smile at her. "My friend wants to know if you'd suck his dick," we say. We laugh big. With our faces. With our bodies. We fall into each other. We fall over the seats.

She moves as far away from us as she can. We have her surrounded. She is trapped in her seat. She pushes against the window as if she could escape. Get out of the train. Tumble onto the tracks. We calm down. Only for the rest of the ride, we call out to her, "Ma'am? Excuse me, ma'am?" so we can laugh some more. When we get off, we can see that the old lady is still scared. That she hates us because we are everything she has tried to deny that we are. We are everything she has thought but has never said.

We have shown her.

CICADA

In the dank of DC's summer heat, cicadas scaled the heights of oak trees, vocal and untrained trapeze artists. But their shells, discarded and crumpled like candy wrappers, clogged drains and littered the sides of the road. The air was smeared with humidity, but as they drove through Rock Creek Park, a breeze lifted and Ellery, her face thrust out of the car window, waited for the wind to hopscotch across her cheeks.

"Stop." Her mother tugged on Ellery's elbow and Ellery lowered her face back into the interior of Ms. Anita's car.

"Lo, she's fine." Her father turned around from the passenger seat. He frowned at her mother and winked at Ellery.

"All these damn bugs. Devils, I tell you," Ms. Anita said. The wheels of her car crushed the dark masses again and again.

On the playground at Ellery's school, a boy picked up

one of the cracked bodies and threw it at the long, full ponytail of a girl. She tried to shake free of it, catching the Holy Ghost far from the aisles of any church, like the one Ellery's mother dragged her to on Sundays. "Get it out! Get it off!" the girl yelled. The giggling bunch of boys ran, but Ellery, with her thumb and forefinger, pulled the bug remains out of the strands of hair.

"My science teacher says they wait underground until they're ready to come out," Ellery said. She tried to lean forward between the seats, but the seat belt pulled her back.

"Your dress," her mother said. She brushed nonexistent bits of lint from the fabric, stiff from dry cleaning. Her mother had insisted that would make it look best for today. It didn't smell like it had been cleaned, not like their clothes after they washed them at the laundromat. Their dryer at home had been broken since last summer. Their washing machine had stopped at Christmas.

"You go all this way for her to take piano?" Ms. Anita asked. "I bet there's somebody right over in Northeast."

"You're probably right, Ms. Anita," Mom answered back. She had to yell so her voice would land on the waiting ears of Ms. Anita instead of the wind taking it out to the trees.

"Too much money over here, you ask me," Ms. Anita said.

"Appreciate this ride, especially today. All of these rides you've given us. We could have just taken the bus—"

"Probably have to take two different ones to get you this far west of the park."

8

"Three," her mother said, but this time she did not yell.

The kids in her neighborhood all hated being west of the park: Woodley Park or Friendship Heights or Ellery's favorite neighborhood (the site of her piano lessons, the site of today's excitement), the Gold Coast. Ellery had no name for the collection of streets around her home where she skinned knees and hands. The houses on the Gold Coast weren't just in rows, obedient toy soldiers. These houses were like gathering up all the toys Ellery had ever owned, the Barbies, the stuffed animals, the building blocks. They had what her mother called turrets or Juliet balconies and front yards big enough for a good game of tag. Even the plain brick ones caused a tightness in Ellery's belly. Some of them had ivy growing up the sides, angling for a way in.

"I don't know how you've been making it without a car—"

"We've been making it fine," her father said.

"Even to the Gold Coast?" Ms. Anita asked. Her father said that Ms. Anita wouldn't believe you even if you said water was wet. When Ellery went over to use Ms. Anita's piano to practice, she would always ask how long it'd be. "Just an hour, Ms. Anita," her mother told her. "About the same time it would take me to do your hair." And then, Ms. Anita, putting a hand to her gelled ponytail, would say, "Well, if it's just an hour . . ."

"Mom, look," Ellery said. "I bet it's cool in there." She reached out to grip her mother's forearm without turning to see where her fingers would land. Ellery could feel

9

drops of sweat down her back like her mother pouring water over her head in the kitchen sink when she got her hair washed, the towel on her neck already good and soaked. The wetness now the stickiness of salt, not the stickiness of conditioner.

"So, this a recital?" Ms. Anita asked. She watched for the answer in her rearview mirror, waiting for Ellery's mother to respond.

"No, it's a competition. Mrs. Hamilton says that's like a recital with prizes," Ellery answered before her mother could.

"Oh yeah? You gonna win?" Ms. Anita asked. She jutted an elbow out to Ellery's father and smiled.

"Yes," Ellery said. When she played the piano, Ellery could find no edges to the world, no start and stop. Not in the music or in the Italian words Mrs. Hamilton used to tell Ellery to slow down or play loudly. The world was there for her. She was just waiting to come out and see it.

★★★

Ms. Anita's car clunked into the circular driveway of the recital hall. It was really a kind of church, a synagogue, her father told them.

"Pretty slick, huh?" Dad said. But Ellery wouldn't have called the building slick, not like the shine on the escalators in the Metro. The white building trimmed in the silver of its four large columns was more like the platter they used only for Thanksgiving and Christmas dinner. Ellery was never allowed to carry it to the table or even pick it up when she served herself turkey. Ms. Anita rounded the corners of the drive and braked her old car in front of the large wooden doors of the synagogue. The cicadas were quieter here.

"Ready?" her father asked. He craned around to smile at Ellery in the back seat. The armpits of his white shirt were already soaked through with sweat. Her mother rubbed her back and Ellery nodded.

"You sure you won't come, Ms. Anita?" Mom asked.

"Got my book club," Ms. Anita said. "But you call me and I'll come back."

Her father opened the car door and Ellery climbed out, trying to keep her legs together like her mother always said, but she couldn't get out of the car like that. She jumped out and landed with a hop on the sidewalk. She made sure not to turn in case disapproval was on her mother's face. Her father grabbed one of her hands, her mother the other, and they walked toward the building. Ms. Anita's car creaked away behind them.

The four doors before them were the dark wood of the banister at Grandma's house that Mom always told her was not meant for messing. Glass above the wood reflected their three bodies back to them, but it would have taken at least six Ellerys stacked on one another for her to reach the top. In the white stone above the glass, somebody had carved two candleholders and one picture of a book with round corners instead of pointy ones. It was better than any Gold Coast house she'd ever seen.

Her father tugged at her hand to get her through one of the doors.

Inside, the ceilings stretched even higher than the glass. It would take even more Ellerys to reach the top. Her shoes echoed on the synagogue's stone floor; each sole striking as if someone were bouncing a ball.

"Sure feels nice in here," Dad said. He wiped his brow with his free hand.

The outstretched arms of smiling women with flowers pinned to the front of their clothes directed them to a red carpeted area in front of more doors. Now, Ellery's shoes couldn't be heard at all, as if she had vanished. There was just one door this time, wide and wooden. Her father grabbed a silver handle and opened it for Ellery to walk through. Her mother held her hand even tighter as if they were about to cross the street.

At the front of this new room, the one where she would perform, was the same rounded book, but bigger and lit up, maybe from a spotlight somewhere Ellery couldn't see. Ellery and her mother belonged to a congregation that was small and, as her father said, too broke to worship anywhere better than a high school cafeteria. The sanctuary was a bunch of metal folding chairs and tables that sometimes had dried ketchup on them. It always smelled of newly opened cans of corn.

Here, the air was like right after her mother vacuumed the carpet. There were no worn-out tables, the ones at the front too beautiful for anybody to ever be allowed to get ketchup near them. Four steps led up to the stage, glowing from the light of the big book and from the gleam of polished wood. To the left side was all that mattered, a piano: grand, white, and gleaming. It was not the old upright at Ms. Anita's or the kind at Mrs. Hamilton's, smaller than this one and black.

Mrs. Hamilton descended from her place on the stage. Her long brown hair was piled on top of her head in a bun. Ellery's mother wore her hair in a bun like that sometimes, but only when she didn't care what her hair looked like. At the stove when she was cooking. When they carried laundry baskets full of clothes to the laundromat. Mrs. Hamilton wasn't about to do laundry or cook a pot of spaghetti. Her hair was messy on purpose. And even though her dress sparkled, golden threads woven into the swirls of deep pink and white, Mrs. Hamilton didn't look dressed up.

"And you're here," Mrs. Hamilton said. Even words that weren't Italian Mrs. Hamilton said as though they were. She had lived in Europe, she told Ellery often. All over Europe. One place in Europe would have been plenty for Ellery, but that it was more than one seemed important to Mrs. Hamilton. Mrs. Hamilton shook Mom's and Dad's hands, clasping their one hand with both of hers, ringed and nail polished. "The parents may sit anywhere they like. Closer is better of course to see the beautiful finger work Signorina Ellery will do."

Her father scanned the half-filled cushioned movie theater seats. "Space right there." He grabbed Ellery's shoulder and shook it. "You'll do great."

"It'll be beautiful. I already know," her mother said. She fished for a comb in her purse and fussed over the front of Ellery's hair. She leaned back to check her work and smiled. Baby powder peeked out from the neckline of her mother's black dress. If Ellery touched it, the whiteness would only spread.

Her father jingled the change in his pocket. "Come on, we don't want to lose those seats."

Her mother stroked Ellery's hair again. Dad put a hand on her back and led her away.

"Shall we meet your competition?" Mrs. Hamilton said.

The other students, some boys, mostly girls, were seated in the first row. A few of them only nodded at her as Mrs. Hamilton went down the line naming those she knew and prompting others to introduce themselves. "Have a seat here." Mrs. Hamilton gestured to an empty seat between two girls, both in cropped, colorful sweaters and spring dresses. Both had stud earrings, and one, when she touched a hand to her tortoiseshell headband, revealed a silver bracelet with a tiny silver tag hanging from it. They sat with their ankles crossed and their hands picking at starched sundress collars. These girls got out of cars with their legs together and their shoes unscuffed.

"I'm Cara," the girl without the bracelet said when Ellery sat down. She wasn't nearly as pretty as the other girl. Mrs. Hamilton clicked away from them in her high heels.

"I'm Ellery," she said. She turned to smile at the other girl too, the one with the bracelet, even though she hadn't yet given her name.

14

"I like your hair," the girl said. She pulled on her blond ponytail, resting it on her shoulder.

Ellery's hair had been pressed that morning. She had begged her mother for months to let her cut it. She would be in junior high soon, she told her, couldn't she be just a little grown now? Her mother finally cut it when she knew Ellery would be in the competition. Ellery felt the ends of her hair and smiled at her.

"I wish my hair were fuller like that. Mine is so fine and lays so flat, but you've got that kind of poof at your roots." The girl widened her eyes when she said *poof*.

Ellery nodded. She felt an ache somewhere her arms were too short to reach.

"Lori!" Cara whisper-shouted before she let escape a small laugh. Her voice snapped to pity when Ellery's hand went to the front of her hair. "She's just like that," Cara assured her.

Lori probably cheated at war and ate all the red Now and Laters in the pack. Lori might have lived in one of those houses that Ellery loved, but she wouldn't last one minute with an alley-glass-skinned knee. She'd have gone home crying to her mother. She wouldn't have gotten right back on her bike and kept riding.

One of the other white women besides Mrs. Hamilton quieted the crowd. Her fingers pressed down on the air as if she were playing all the keys of the piano at once.

Ellery turned to search for the faces of her parents, but she could no longer tell, even in the swarm of white bodies, which bodies she belonged to. She thought she saw her mother's hair between the gelled heads of two suited white men, but when she leaned her head back to make sure, Lori hissed at her.

"Your teacher's looking at you. You better pay attention," Lori said. Ellery tilted forward, sitting straighter in her seat so she wouldn't disappoint Mrs. Hamilton. When she glanced Mrs. Hamilton's way though, she wasn't watching Ellery, only the stage. "Maybe she was looking somewhere else," Lori said. She shrugged her shoulders.

Ellery placed her folded hands in her lap just like Lori and tried to hold her knees together through the songs of the youngest kids, all of the tunes short, in four-four time, and played allegro, joyful and fast.

Finally, Ellery's age group began to play. Each pianist (Mrs. Hamilton said Ellery should call herself that) in their turn going up to the stage, having their piece announced, and then setting off, waiting for their fingers to remember all the movements that had been drilled into them for weeks. Some of them had played in competitions before, Mrs. Hamilton told her at her lessons. But it didn't mean they were any better than her and even those who had won had no advantage: "Winning once doesn't mean you will win again," Mrs. Hamilton said.

Lori went up to play and Ellery let her knees go limp and her ankles uncross. A woman announced the title of Lori's piece and before she sat at the bench, Lori raised a shoulder and a smile for the audience, who complimented this preperformance with louder applause than the girl before her had received at the end of her song. From head to toe, Lori was a new Mary Jane shoe fresh out of the box, buffed to a shine so you could see your own reflection in it, but all lopsided and weird. The squeeze and hurt of it. Still, Ellery also longed for pretty things. She clapped, but with her hands still in her lap.

The Italian words resounded in Lori's playing. *Forte* when it should be. *Piano* when it was best. Lori might really know those words, maybe she had been all over Europe like Mrs. Hamilton. Lori's finger positioning was precise, her hands arched as if tennis balls rested under her palms. It was the way Mrs. Hamilton wanted Ellery to play, but Ellery's hands sometimes fell a little flat, perched too low.

"Hey," Cara said, poking Ellery's still-folded hands. From the side of the stage, this time Mrs. Hamilton *was* looking at her and motioning with both hands for Ellery to come. Standing, Ellery would have the best chance to see her parents, but looking behind her might mean tripping over something. She walked toward Mrs. Hamilton, never turning around and with her hands clasped in front of her.

"Go up and wait." Mrs. Hamilton gently pushed at Ellery's back. She walked up the three steps to the stage, concealed from the audience by velvet curtains. Ellery could focus on Lori's face now, the way she couldn't sitting right next to her. Her nose was smaller than Ellery's. Her cheeks the pink of watermelon candy, a color that would have been muted on Ellery's dark skin. Lori's ponytail flounced as she played, as excited to be there with her as the rest of the audience was. She was pretty good, but maybe church just made music better.

Sometimes on Sundays, Ellery's mother would raise a hand and wave it during a song. Once after service, Ellery asked her why she did that. All her mother would say is that she felt full. Ellery thought of the discomfort of too many hamburgers or one scoop too many of ice cream, but her mother's full—a hand at her heart and the dots of tears at the corners of her eyes—was different. "All I feel just comes out," she told Ellery.

Lori finished, and when she rose from the bench and bowed, the audience clapped happily. Three people in the front wrote on sheets of paper, the judges, she now remembered Mrs. Hamilton whispering to her on the walk to her seat. A row of well-dressed white people stood up, clapping louder than the rest. Lori exited the stage and came toward Ellery. Lori looked like she might speak, but only poked her lips out at Ellery and pulled her wandering ponytail back to its place on her shoulder.

The woman announced Ellery's piece and extended her hand to invite Ellery to start playing. Ellery moved out of the shadows of the curtains and stood before the audience. She started to bow, but she did it slowly hoping during her bending she would finally see her parents, but she couldn't find them. She wasn't even sure where her own seat was anymore. The distance from her to the piano grew, but Ellery imagined this was Ms. Anita's house, the same shaky wooden bench, the same smell of bleach and Vaseline, her mother just starting on Ms. Anita's hair.

Ellery sat at the keys and placed the tips of her fingers

on the ivories. She lightly stroked them. Then, she finally pressed down and played the opening chord. She loved the way it sounded. Her fingers raced across the keys to the next chord. *Too fast*, she heard Mrs. Hamilton say in her head as she would in practice. Ellery slowed and pressed each note so every one would be heard. She chanted Italian words, whispering them to herself. Most had nothing to do with her song, but the melody of them made her want to do her best. The notes played well together, and those notes led to new notes, which led to other notes. Ellery didn't know if this piano was better or if this church, this synagogue, where music played that made people feel full, was doing the same for her music, but she felt it. She felt full. Or maybe she felt just out of the dirt, out from underground and into the summer sun. She touched the last of the notes, her fingers light on them, *piano*, and then off of them and back into her lap.

She heard the clapping before she stood up all the way, before she turned around and took her bow. And then she saw them, her parents standing up like Lori's had. Her father yelling and calling out her name. Her mother wasn't clapping, but she had a hand to her heart. Cara was waiting to play and could only stare at Ellery. At the bottom of the three stairs, Mrs. Hamilton leaned toward Ellery and touched the side of her face. "Beautiful," she told her. Ellery smiled. Some people were still clapping, some people who weren't even her parents. Ellery walked back to her seat. Lori didn't say anything, didn't even give her a smile. Ellery sat and Cara played, but even though the room was filled with as much sound as before, Ellery heard nothing over the thump of her heartbeat.

★★★

They announced the winners for the younger kids first, the third prize and the second. The first-prize winner, a boy with blue pants, a pinstriped shirt, and a bow-tie, ran up when they called his name. His parents took pictures, and he smiled and posed until they said he could stop. The woman who had introduced all of them stepped back to the microphone after the little boy finally left the stage. She thanked everyone for coming and then began to thank a long list of other people.

"You were really good," Cara whispered to Ellery. Ellery smiled, but didn't thank her, wary of daggers of giggles that might follow.

"Any *thing* can make noise," Lori said.

"You were really good, like really good," Cara said again without a giggle or a smile to diminish her words.

"For our nine-to-twelve age group, we had some excellent competitors representing many parts of the city. Our judges had a difficult task, but we chose three pianists we think excelled today."

She paused, and Ellery didn't want to hope too hard that her name would come out of her mouth. "In third place and winning one hundred dollars, Bobby McMillan."

From the other side of the crowd, a boy Ellery hadn't

even remembered playing went up. He shook the woman's hand up and down and up and down until she took her hand away to give him two stiff pieces of paper, a certificate and a check.

"And, in second place, with a piece that showed real technique by a pianist who exhibited great poise—that's the importance of this competition too, not just playing music, but turning these kids into true ladies and gentlemen."

Ellery didn't know if she had been ladylike enough for this woman or if she had "great poise."

"Our second-place prize of two hundred fifty dollars goes to Lori Hansen."

"See," Lori breathed out before she went forward to claim her trophy and check. She curtsied for the audience and they clapped harder.

Lori came back to Ellery's side and hissed, "Can't imagine you'll be able to top that."

"And our first-prize winner in our nine-to-twelve age group is someone who really surprised the judges . . ." The woman stopped, building urgency, and Ellery knew her mother was in the audience saying to her father, "Why don't she get on with it?" Ellery wanted her to, but then she didn't because she might not have won and then she would have to turn to this girl next to her and say something about her winning, not because she really wanted to, but because she would want her to know her parents had taught her well.

Ellery took in a deep breath to either help her say "Thank you" to the judges or "Congratulations" to Lori.

"The winner is Ellery Cook."

Ellery heard a squeal from the audience. She walked up the steps of the stage and to the waiting woman. The fullness of playing multiplied, winning all the marbles in a game of jacks, seeing a tree full of cicadas where it seemed at first there was just one. The trophy was just a note, a musical note, mounted on a stone stand, but on that stand were the words *First Place*. But what Ellery really wanted was the $500 check.

The woman smiled and handed it to her. "Congratulations."

Ellery didn't shake her hand like the boy had and she didn't curtsy. Her smile and thank-you were so small, they ended up being only for herself. She descended the stairs of the stage to more congratulations and compliments on her playing. Everyone was standing up, kids finding their parents and parents finding their joyous or disappointed child.

Lori and Cara were just past the last step. Ellery fingered her first-place trophy and Lori fingered the careful pleats of her dress.

"Winning is just for fun," Lori said.

"It was fun," Ellery said. "How I won."

The watermelon candy at Lori's cheeks darkened.

Out of the clusters of people, Ellery's parents emerged. Her father whooping and letting loose emphatic one-word sentences. "Yes." "Right." "Winner." Ellery could see from her mother's swollen eyes that she had been crying.

"This one," Mrs. Hamilton said, floating toward them and pointing at Ellery, "did magnificently well."

"We thought so too," Dad said. He patted Ellery's head, mussing her hair until she allowed a smile to escape.

"It was so beautiful. The song," her mother said. "I've heard her play it, but—"

"She played it better today than she ever has," Mrs. Hamilton said. "You like your prize?"

Ellery nodded, renewing her grip on the trophy. She moved away from her parents so she could present the check. She wanted to do it just like the lady on the lottery drawing. "Here. It's for the car. We won't have to take the bus," Ellery said. She unfolded her arm and let the peach-colored paper dangle from her fingertips.

Her mother glanced at Mrs. Hamilton and then squatted down in front of Ellery. She placed her hand under one curled side of Ellery's hair. "Honey, it's a savings bond."

The bond was stiffer than cash or a check, but Ellery didn't know why that made a difference. She searched her father's face for the answer.

"See, baby, that number it has? That five hundred? Well, it's worth something it's not really worth yet. But by the time you go to college, by then, what it says it's worth, it'll be worth," her father said.

"Don't you worry about a car. This is yours," her mother said. She pushed Ellery's hair behind her ear, only to pull it back out again. Grooming her even though her moment was over.

"Oh." Ellery dropped the hand with the bond down to her side.

"You kind of have to believe it'll get to be worth that

in time," her father said. He put a hand on Mom's back and she straightened back to her height. Ellery looked no one in the eye.

"You won, remember?" Mrs. Hamilton said, her voice in a sharp key. "Smile."

* * *

They waited in the circular driveway for Ms. Anita to come. From the trees, the cicadas were deafening the street, before they would be gone for seventeen more years. By then, Ellery would be grown and the $500 savings bond would finally be worth its face value. Her parents chattered along with the cicadas. They told her how proud they were and how beautiful her playing was. Mom couldn't wait to tell the other members of the choir, and Dad couldn't wait to tell everybody he knew.

Lori and her family came out through the dark, wooden doors. Ellery tightened her grip on the trophy and savings bond. The people who had stood up and cheered for Lori surrounded her now. Two men in suits and two ladies in grown-up versions of the dress Lori had on. The group walked around Ellery's family, but Lori came closer than the others, brushing past Ellery's mother, her pink cashmere cardigan nudging the polyester of her mother's dress. Her mother turned toward Lori and her family.

"Congratulations," Lori said. The family members nodded their approval of Lori's word.

"Say thank you, Ellery," her mother said. Ellery

squeezed her mother's hand, but did not speak. Her mother smiled at Lori and found the faces of the adults. "Your daughter. She was wonderful."

"Yes, thank you." The woman had Lori's face, but no watermelon candy at her cheeks. Hair that might once have been pulled into a coveted ponytail lay on her shoulders, straightened and brightly blond. On one wrist was a bracelet with the same small tag that Lori's had and a ring with a stone so far from her finger it seemed suspended in midair. Her dress looked as if it had been dry-cleaned. No sweat ringed her underarms. There was no baby powder to be found.

"That dress is very pretty," her mother said. She always knew how much things cost without looking at price tags. "Slow down," she would tell Ellery, "don't splash water on that lady," she might say, "that dress cost her good money." "Don't kick that dirt up around that man, his suit is more than I make in a week."

"Thank you." The woman took Lori's hand and turned away from Ellery's mother.

They walked to a car nearby, silver like the synagogue's columns. The car's horn beeped and one of the men opened the front door for the woman holding Lori's hand. The man opened the door for Lori next. Lori turned back and smiled. Her teeth were so straight, white fence posts lined up and freshly painted. She smoothed out the back of her skirt and sat down. The man closed the door behind her and all Ellery could see of Lori through the window was the pink of her face and the blond of her ponytail.

"Now, that's a beautiful thing right there. Never seen that model in that color," her father said. He leaned down and said very near Ellery's ear, "One day soon, we'll be riding in that."

Other car doors closed, slammed. The cicadas only got louder.

Lori's car started to take off, going around the circular driveway of the synagogue. Ellery dropped her mother's hand and walked toward the departing car, quickening her steps when the wheels began to spin faster. When her legs couldn't keep up, she bent down and picked up the shells of the cicadas, pushed to the side in gutters and broken under indifferent wheels. She hurled the black bodies at the windows of the car. She ran now, her Mary Janes pinching. She picked up more cicada shells, throwing two or three at a time and then three or four more. She threw all the shells she could find, even when the car pulled out of the driveway. She was breathing fast by the time she stopped running at the end of the drive, still holding a couple of cicada shells in her hand. She walked back toward the synagogue, turning around as she went to see how far away the car was.

"Did you see?" Ellery asked her parents. Ellery breathed out and smiled. "Did you?"

EVERYTHING SHE WANTS

Alexis carries a bag that is too heavy for her to the car. She puts it down after the first set of stairs and drags sticky peanut-butter-and-jelly fingers over the sweat gathering on the back of her neck. She heaves it the rest of the way, setting the bulk of the bundle on her leg. No one else is ready to go to Ocean City, but she is. She can't find the dark pink swimsuit that she and her father bought at Hecht's, but she'll wear her old one, the babyish one, with the rainbows.

Alexis is eight and is ready for real life to begin.

Inside the two-story colonial in Northeast, her mother is putting chicken salad sandwiches into plastic zip-top bags and burying two cream sodas for Alexis and two root beers for her father in the store-bought ice in the foam cooler. Alexis wants to do nice things for her mother, but she doesn't go back inside to help. She wants to wait by the car until they leave so she is one step closer to the water and wearing sunglasses on the beach like grown women do. She wears her mother's perfume sometimes. On special days, her mother lets her. Today, Alexis sneaks it. She likes to spray one wrist and press the thin skin to as many parts of her body as she can. Later, when her father sprays her with sunscreen the smells will mix and Alexis will fall asleep on the beach blanket with her wrist pressed to her nose.

Her mother packed fashion magazines and Alexis is going to take one out of her bag when her mother takes a nap in the sun almost as soon as they arrive. Alexis thinks those small women in the magazines are so very pretty and she knows why her mom flips through them over and over again some days.

"She doesn't need this much stuff," her father says when Alexis gets the bag to the curb in front of their house.

"A woman has needs," Alexis says, and her father's forehead troubles itself even though he smiles at her. He reaches out to grab Alexis's cheek. They are fat, too fat for her face. Alexis knows that those cheeks are part of what's stopping her from being a woman.

"I suppose so," he says. He reaches down to scratch his leg beneath the long white socks he's worn with his khaki shorts.

Alexis doesn't know what a woman needs. Makeup, she could guess, and dresses that other women think are pretty. Her mother likes those things, although she hardly ever wears makeup and she wears too-big T-shirts, staying in that bed for too long. Alexis heard her mother say to her father that she can't help that she needs time to herself. Her father did not say anything back because he saw Alexis standing in the doorway to the dining room right after her mother spoke. He reached out for her instead of her mother and her mother went back upstairs without another word.

Alexis has two best friends in school. Caitlin is white, one of the only ones at Alexis's elementary school, and she wears lip gloss already and tries to sing like a pop star. Nia is like Alexis, but darker, a brown that deepens, while Alexis only gets golden playing in the summer sun. Alexis, Caitlin, and Nia have sleepovers every weekend, and they switch whose house they go to, but Nia's house is the best. It has the biggest yard and Nia's mom is the best cook. But Caitlin's mom orders pepperoni pizza.

Alexis's dad cooked dinner the slumber party before last. It was spaghetti from a jar, and Nia didn't finish eating what was on her plate. Later, in the yellow bedroom with the canopy bed that Alexis's mother had gotten for her special order, she told Alexis that her mother said that no good mother would feed her family from a jar. Alexis hadn't said anything back to her, only turned on her side away from Nia. Caitlin was already asleep.

"What else should we take?" her father asks. He closes the trunk before Alexis can answer. He sits in the passenger seat, his long legs resting on the crisp cut grass in front of their house. Alexis wants long legs like him one day. Then, she can be in those magazines. He pats his lap and Alexis sits. Her shoes are off and she tucks her toes behind her father's knees. He nuzzles the top of her head. She has braids today that her mother did. It is the first time her mother's done her hair in months.

Alexis wants to ask a question her mother won't have to know about. It is a question that Alexis will in some way end up asking for the rest of her life: Will she always be sad? But the question is rough in her mouth and she can't swallow it and she can't spit it out. So, it sits between her teeth and her tongue, undissolved, unsoftened no matter how much saliva she runs over it.

"Are you okay?" he asks into her hair.

Alexis nods, and when her father grabs for her cheek again and asks what she's storing in them to make them so chubby, the question dislodges and tumbles down her throat, lost for the rest of her childhood.

Her mother walks out of the house carrying the cooler and her father stands up to let Alexis off of his lap, and he takes the steps to the house two at a time to remove the burden from the hands of her mother. He says things to her that Alexis cannot hear. One day Alexis will look back and be sure that one of the things a woman needs is love.

"Do we have everything?" her father asks and walks down the stone steps. He puts the cooler on the back seat of their station wagon. He helps her mother into the front seat, slow to let go of her hand. Alexis lands with a joyous thump on the back seat and closes the door so fast she almost catches her fingers. Her braids clatter together, Alexis's whole body full of excitement and exhaustion that they are going somewhere and that her mother is happy today.

They will ride through the neighborhood and out of DC into Maryland with the windows down. The breeze will be strong and thick. When they park, after rolling through sand, right in front of all that water, the breeze won't be in the car anymore. It will be everywhere and Alexis will want to go and run everywhere with it. She will look through the front windshield to see just how high the waves are.

On the beach, their towels finally laid out, she will hold her mother's hand even though her mother takes too long to walk to the water. But when it is right, Alexis will release the dry warmth of her mother's hand and tumble into the wet of the surf. One day, when she is all grown with a little girl of her own and days when she must stay in bed, she will remember her toes sinking into sand and know that this, too, is a kind of solid ground.

STRONG MEN

The backyard could not contain the celebration, too joyous to be boxed in by the honeysuckle and hedges at its perimeter. People must have heard them far down the block, all the way to the junior high school where Bit's older brother, Ronnie, liked to shoot hoops. She couldn't remember this many people at their house before, but they had never had an event as important as Ronnie graduating from high school. Family from out of town, church folks, her dad's coworkers, all of them were asking questions about what was next for Ronnie and whether thirteen was old enough for Bit to have a boyfriend. She focused on covering the weathered teak table in the center of the yard with old copies of the *Washington Post* so she wouldn't have to answer questions or get her cheeks pinched.

After the partygoers ate crabs, the papers would all get destroyed, wadded at the end of the meal into grocery bags and put into the garbage bins that night to contain the smell of the sea gone bad. Last summer, her father had stopped midwhack at a claw and read off a headline to her, Ronnie, and their mother: U.S. DEFENDS POLICY TOWARD SOUTH AFRICA.

Ronnie would want to see today's sports section, so he could read what they were saying about the draft and his favorite, Len Bias, their hometown boy and a certified star, going as a first-round pick. "That Jordan kid from UNC," her father said, "had nothing on Bias." But Bit couldn't find Ronnie in the crowd of people. He had grown in the last year, nearly taller than their father, but still she could not spot his broadening shoulders or newly mustached face.

A voice behind her said, "I thought there would be more boys here."

Bit hadn't seen her best friend, Callie, walk in, but once there, she was hard to ignore. Callie, who could do Janet Jackson's entire dance from the "What Have You Done for Me Lately" video and walked through the halls of their junior high school sliding her feet and shrugging her shoulders to music that wasn't playing.

Callie pulled at Bit's hand to get her to sit down on the teak table and pushed aside some of the carefully laid layers of newsprint. "One week of school left. So, what are we doing this summer?" Callie asked.

Bit was more focused on the plans for her plate. Her father had finished grilling a batch of hamburgers and the ribs were getting their first turn above the hot coals. Bit reached for a plate from the foam stack, but Callie pushed her hands away and shook her head. "Janet doesn't eat ribs."

"Well, I need to read all those books for next year," Bit said. Their English teacher had given them a mimeograph of the ninth-grade reading list and Bit's hands had been stamped with the chemical smell of the copy the rest of the day.

"You don't say things like that to Derrick, do you?" Callie asked. She tightened her side ponytail. Derrick was sixteen, a high school boy Bit had mumbled an introduction to a few weeks ago. He had dimples and long fingers that played with the straps of his backpack. "You got some pretty eyes," he'd said to her one day after school. Ever since, she had slowed on the walk from their junior high to the Metro, past the high school and the kids who hung out in front of the building, hoping Derrick was among them.

Above all the noise, the rusted back screen door screeched and Bit's mother came out. She deposited hefty bowls of food on a long table off to the side. Bit looked to Callie, but she still shook her head no. Bit's mother wore a white cotton dress, her hips accentuated by the flounce of the skirt. The color of it made her skin look even browner. Bit wished she were her mother's shade, but Callie had told her no, she didn't. "Light-skinned girls get more guys," Callie liked to say, something her mother believed. Callie and her mother were both light skinned, but Callie reassured Bit that she was at least on the lighter side of brown.

Her mother crossed the yard and there, finally, was Ronnie, with the skin tone of their mother and the lean angles of their father. He was a junior, Ronnie to his father's Ron. Someone called out to Ronnie and his mother to smile for a picture. The flash went off and the picture shot out of the front of the camera, a tongue teasing anyone watching. Ronnie fanned the picture back and forth. Mom and Ronnie leaned in to take a look.

"Crabs," her father yelled from the front of the yard. He came toward where Bit and Callie were still sitting, until Bit pulled on Callie's arm to get her up.

He dumped the cooked crabs onto the middle of the table. A rumble went through the crowd, and people sat down to get a good spot and grab what they wanted. Her mother went inside and quickly returned to set down bowls at every other seat. Bit didn't even have to look to know that melted butter and hot sauce was inside. Each person set to work on their first crabs, still seemingly alive until their shells were pried off and they were exposed as only dinner. They dug into the crabs' insides and took out the spongy fingers and the smear of yellow everyone called the mustard. Some cracked the crab down the center. Others started pulling off the legs. Some of them had mallets, careful to pound the shells with the right pressure. Too much and they would be left with crabmeat flecked with inedible crunch. Others used their teeth, more precise tools, to get inside. Those who were skilled impressed each other with chunks of sweet, white crabmeat pulled whole and intact from their dark red containers. Once the rhythm set in, they could go back to their stories, their long swigs of beer, their joyous bites of corn on the cob. Eating crabs was summer magic as far as Bit was concerned.

When they were younger, Ronnie would coax Bit into the bathroom to see the crabs snapping and clawing to get out of the bathtub. "They're trapped," Ronnie would say. He would hold out a pencil to the large gray-blue creatures. They never seemed alive, more like those animatronic toys her father had gotten her for Christmas one year. Those creatures moved because they were supposed to, not because they made the choice. Her mother lined the porcelain sides of the bathtub with garbage bags now, even after all these years of scrapes and scratches. Bit would rub the nicks on the sides of the tub with her big toe whenever she showered, waiting for this point in the summer to come. One year, a couple of crabs got loose, dumped haphazardly by her father. Their low bodies grazed the ground. Bit could have kicked them, even if she couldn't have crushed their shells with her tennis shoes, but instead she ran, screaming and laughing. Ronnie laughed too, and she remembered hearing under his repeating of her name ("Bit. Bit, it's fine.") that he too had been afraid of them for reasons that didn't make any sense.

Ronnie still looked out for her, but now when Bit asked him to kill the bug or explain the song or tell her why that street or that neighborhood wasn't safe, he would say, "I won't always do this." Come August, he would be away at college, but since he would be at Howard, he wouldn't be far. Or, maybe that wasn't how it would be.

"Bit," her mother called out. Bit located her mother's voice in the back of the yard, her face smiling and her hand beckoning in the middle of the mounting darkness.

"Come say hello to some people." Bit reluctantly walked away from Callie and toward a collection of chairs in the opposite corner of the yard. Her mother gripped her arm. "My younger one," she said to the group. Bit had seen all the faces before, so they had probably seen her and knew who she was, but she didn't know their names. Her mother pointed to each person and told Bit why she should remember Ms. This, That, and the Third. Bit didn't listen, bored already. She wanted to go back to Callie. "Sit down," her mother said, tugging on her arm. Bit perched on the edge of the wrought-iron bench's cushion. Callie had wandered over to Ronnie. She said something to him and his fist lightly tagged her shoulder.

"I still don't know how she got to be thirteen," her mother said, touching Bit's jaw. Bit wanted to wrinkle her face in annoyance, but her mother wouldn't like that. "Sit back." Her mother pressed a hand into Bit's shoulder to move her closer to the seat.

"You never do know," one of the women said. She was all gray, someone's grandmother.

"You don't know even how you got to be old," another woman said and the group endorsed her with drawn-out affirmations.

"I still remember when Ron and I first met. When we first slow danced," her mother said. Bit snuck a look at her mother, avoiding eye contact so she wouldn't think she was really listening. Her mother's face was even prettier with her cheeks softened.

"Uh-oh, she's about to tell us too much." The other women broke into laughter and Bit's mother followed.

"You just never know that's the start of your future. Page one."

"And how's that book turning out?" one of the women asked.

"Well, there's been some plot twists and turns," her mother said. More laughter and affirmation from the women; one yelled out, "Always are." Bit's mother stroked Bit's hair and she finally sat all the way back to lie on the cotton of her mother's dress. "But, I think the story's coming out pretty well. Pretty well. That boy came hurdling out. Ronnie. I mean, hurdling. Sprinting and jumping just to make it out. And now."

"She'll be on her way soon, too."

"Before I know it. Nothing makes you feel more powerful and more powerless than parenthood. Here, you made these children, but one day you won't be able to do anything about what happens to them." Bit was used to being talked about as if she wasn't sitting right there, but saying what she often said to her parents ("I'm right here.") would have been rude.

"Amen."

"But, you can only hope and pray."

"Only ever."

"I mean they're gonna go out and raise some hell. Just like we did." They all laughed, a ripple going through the group and then dissolving into a shimmering quiet.

"Just as long as they know how to get out of that hell."

"Just as long as they do."

Since only Callie was here, Bit didn't feel ashamed to lean on her mother and let her stroke her hair. For a minute, she closed her eyes and the voices of the party blanketed her. When her lids slid back open, Callie was in a different corner, closer to them and talking to Derrick.

Bit sat up as if struck.

"What's wrong?" her mother asked. Bit shook her head, but her mother frowned.

"I forgot I was supposed to get Daddy something." Bit stood up and walked the long way around the group toward Callie and Derrick.

Her hands went to her hair and then her T-shirt and jeans to make sure she didn't look like a bama. She wanted to go and talk to him, stare at his dimples, match up her first name with his last name while he talked, but she hadn't thought enough about what to say. Ronnie said most of his friends weren't coming. The friends who had—girls who her mother asked why they thought high heels were right for a backyard cookout—Bit definitely wouldn't talk to. They wore dark lipstick and big earrings only slightly covered by their asymmetrical haircuts. Bit had asked her mother if she could get her hair cut like that and her mother had laughed: "So people can think you got some kind of neck defect?"

Callie was getting a new cut next week and even though she hadn't worn makeup today, in case Bit's mother told on her, Derrick probably liked talking to her. Boys got a shine in their eyes when they talked to Callie. Their fingers reached for the corner of her denim jacket or sometimes they'd throw a long arm around her shoulders, a hand dangling at the side of her breast. Derrick wasn't touching her though, and when Bit finally walked up to them, Callie smiled as she approached and said, "Oh, look who it is."

Callie could be so obvious. She would push Bit into cute boys on the Metro and wait for Bit to blush and mumble an apology. She kept telling Bit that boys didn't mind that kind of stuff: "Obvious is better with them."

Bit stepped closer, stuffing her hands in her back pockets. "Um, hey."

Derrick smiled and the dimples showed themselves. "Your mom threw down on those crabs."

"You ate some?" Bit asked. He had been there longer than she realized. She hoped he hadn't seen her like a baby in her mother's arms.

"Just a little. You get your fill?" he asked.

"Bit hardly eats anything," Callie said.

"No? I kind of like a girl who would suck on a rib bone," he said. He tucked something behind his ear, something white, and then leaned back in the plastic chair.

"Bit can do that. She'll suck on anything." Callie raised an eyebrow at Derrick and laughed.

"Oh yeah?" Derrick said. He smiled with all his teeth.

"No, I won't." Bit's whole body flushed with shame. Callie was being gross.

"Not even a rib bone? A chicken wing?" he said. He leaned forward again. The dimples reappeared, the wicked smile gone.

"I did want a rib, but I haven't gotten one," Bit said.

"Why don't I go get you one?" Derrick stood. Bit relaxed and met his smile with her own.

"I'll go and get it," Callie said. "I want another soda anyway and you can sit here, Bit." Callie rose and walked off before either of them could stop her.

"She's your best friend or what?" Derrick asked. Bit sat down. She pressed her hands into her thighs, hoping the shake in her fingers would subside.

"Yeah, she's my best friend. Since elementary school," Bit said. She had a drawer full of origamied notes they had passed to each other over the years.

"Dangerous right there," he said. Callie was digging into the cooler, her butt in the air and her hair falling into a curly curtain that shielded her face. He put his focus back on Bit. "I can't stay long, but your brother is my ace, so I had to come."

Derrick had never been over to the house before. Ronnie had never said he was meeting him for a movie. If they were that close, she might have to tell Ronnie she liked Derrick.

"It's gonna be a good summer," Derrick said. He held out his soda to her, but Bit waved it away. He moved it closer and finally she took the cool metal in her hand. Drinking after him must mean something. Boys offered Callie things all the time.

"Yeah." Bit took a small sip from his cream soda until she could figure out something else to say, but Derrick didn't seem to mind the short answer.

"It's like this summer I have it all. I'll get my permit. I can go wherever." Derrick nodded to himself, a slow dip of his chin. He took back the can and drained it. He dropped the empty container onto the grass and stomped it with his extra-white tennis shoes. Callie had moved around the group where Bit's mother was, behind a tree in the back. Bit could see her, but Derrick probably couldn't. Callie gave Bit a big smile and Bit mimicked her. Callie leaned forward and pointed to her chest, motioning for Bit to follow. Bit leaned forward a little until she gazed down and saw vast flat terrain and sat up straight again. "And, I got money," Derrick said, pulling a wad of bills from his pocket. They weren't folded, some were even crumpled and Derrick struggled to straighten out the papers. "We'll go out."

"Okay," Bit said. Callie puckered her lips at Bit, who thought she was loud enough that everyone in the noisy yard could hear her kissing sounds.

"Dope," he said. He stood, adjusted his striped polo, and put a hand to his fade.

"Okay, bye," Bit said. Nerdiness descended as the words left her and Derrick didn't say anything back. He walked away, a slouch from his shoulders to his knees. He found Ronnie in a shadowed corner. Callie came back, with no ribs but wanting every word of what she missed.

From the center of the yard, her father yelled, "Before it gets too late." The crowd settled to a quiet, halting their conversations or finishing them in whispers. "I just wanted to say a little something about why we're all here. My boy, Ronnie? Where's Ronnie?" He pivoted in place searching. Bit was fixated on Ronnie's frame from across the yard. He had heard their father and stood straighter now, his muscles answering the summons. Their father called him a couple of times, until finally one of their father's friends nudged him out of the shadows, unshrouding him. The whole crowd clapped. "Come here," Dad said. Ronnie moved over to Dad, he smiling as much as Ronnie was unsmiling. "This is my boy. And as of yesterday, this is my boy who graduated high school." Cheers came from the corners of the yard; a few raised their beer bottles, whistled, or shouted. "I could not be prouder of him. He'll be a man on Howard's campus this fall. A college man. And, I know that is just the start of all kinds of greatness for this boy. Not just because he's mine, although that helps." Her father's friends laughed, their own love of their sons deep in their throats. "But he will be great because there is no other choice. There is no other possible path for him in life. So, I know he's gonna follow it and that four years from now, we're gonna have an even bigger celebration when he graduates summa cum laude." Ronnie twisted out an expression, the one he gave when he had to suffer through a long talk with their father. He still stood straight, even with the hopes of the crowd and the heavy hand of their father on his back.

"Thank you for coming," Ronnie said. The crowd clapped again, glad he was polite, hopeful that their own boys would be that polite. Bit wanted Ronnie to look at her, so she could make him smile. Ronnie stared out into the yard, past Bit and Callie, past even their mother and her friends. Something in the alley held his attention, a thing past the borders of their yard. Bit followed his gaze. Nothing was there, nothing more than ever was—trash bins, some broken bottles, and the overgrown yard of their neighbors across the way. She turned back. His eyes had left the distance and finally found Bit's face. She gave him a crooked smile to make him laugh. But he didn't, and soon Bit's cheeks dropped.

Eventually, the music slowed and so did the drinking. A halting procession formed as partygoers lingered on their way out, wanting one more laugh or one more word from the summer night. Before long, everyone, even Callie, left for their own homes and whatever plans they had for the duration of the darkness.

Then, it was just the four of them again, just Bit and her family. Together, they cleaned up, wadded the newspapers, packed away food that hadn't been eaten or taken, and Ronnie and her father stuffed trash bag after trash bag. Under the overhead light of the kitchen, her parents kissed, her father's hands low on her mother's back and her hands curved around his neck. Bit walked through the kitchen to the upstairs, but her noise couldn't interrupt their communion. She hoped now she could be alone with Ronnie, but he was already in his bedroom, behind a closed door. Bit climbed into bed, sunned and stuffed. From Ronnie's room, music kicked up, the insistent thump of Run DMC, and Bit didn't bother to bang on the wall for him to turn it down.

***

Callie had a television in her bedroom, a whole stack of *Seventeen* magazines, and a mother who always knocked before she walked in. So, Bit spent long hours at Callie's after school. It had been that way for years. A couple of weeks ago, Callie missed her stop and said she might as well just ride to Bit's stop. The next time, she got off at Bit's stop and said maybe she'd come over for a little while. Today, she didn't pretend she had missed her stop. She didn't bother to say she would only stay for a little while.

"Ronnie going to Howard is gonna be good for us. If things with Derrick don't work, we can always skip high school boys and go straight to college ones. You just gotta figure out how to be what a man wants," Callie said. "My mom says that. She's watching that new black talk show lady all the time now."

"Okay, so what do they want?" Bit asked.

Callie took out mascara and applied it to her lashes. Bit had used it once, but Ronnie called her spider eyes after she forgot to take it off before she got home. Callie had real makeup, a bag for it all the size of a pencil case to hide it from her mother. Bit only snuck lip gloss sometimes in the palest of pinks so her mom couldn't tell.

"I don't know. My mom keeps asking my dad. Maybe when he gives her an answer, he'll move back in," Callie said.

"Maybe."

Callie had designer jeans and makeup, but she no longer had her father in her house. "We couldn't both have parents who were still together," Callie told her the day it happened. "Something was definitely weird about that." A lot of their friends' parents were divorced or together in the same house but with a father who slept in the basement. Some had parents who had never been together or fathers they had never known. Callie's father always had his goatee trimmed and wore polo shirts just tight enough to show he didn't have a gut like other fathers, like Bit's. He wore cologne and had a deep laugh, and Callie's mother, who got her hair done every two weeks and always wore heels, liked to keep her hand on his arm.

All afternoon, they gossiped and shout-giggled until her mother yelled up to them to come down and help with dinner. Callie didn't know how to chop an onion and she always kept the electric beaters too high in the bowl until mashed potatoes flecked the wall beside her. Mom just let Callie sit, positioned by the open doorway, inspecting the dirt under her nails. She stayed that way until Bit's father walked in the front door. Callie leapt up and left the kitchen like Bit would have when she was younger, eager to wrap her arms around his solidness.

"Dinner will be ready soon," Bit heard Callie say. Dad monotoned a response.

Bit's mother leaned back for a better look at the entryway.

"Her mother knows she's coming here all this time?" she asked. She straightened and returned her focus to washing the lettuce in the kitchen sink.

"I guess," Bit said. But Callie's mother hardly knew anything, only what Callie told her and that was never much.

"She should know, Bit," her mother said. Callie laughed

from the living room, the laugh she let boys have when she noticed they smiled too much around her.

"Okay," Bit said.

"She should know so they can talk."

"She's just hanging out," Bit said, trying to edge out the disrespect that had crept into her voice.

"Has she seen her father?"

"I don't know. Maybe." Bit's mother was silent so she instead filled the room with the clatter of stacking plates and silverware for the table.

"Tell your brother dinner is ready" was all her mother finally said. Bit started up the stairs and then heard: "And she shouldn't spend the night." Bit didn't respond so she could pretend she hadn't heard her. Her mother might make Callie go anyway, but maybe if she stayed just late enough, past *The A-Team* and halfway through *Moonlighting*, her mother might give in for the night.

Bit knocked on Ronnie's door. Like Callie's mother, it was what she always did now. She had been yelled at too many times. She knocked again, louder, but he still didn't answer. The only response was more volume on his tape deck, loud enough that everyone in the house probably could have made out the lyrics to "Raising Hell." She banged on the door, the softest parts of her fist able to hit the hardest. She remembered what would get him to turn the music down and open the door.

"The draft," she said, putting her mouth to the door so he would hear. "The draft," she said again. "The draft!" she yelled. Halfway through her yelling the music stopped and he opened the door. "The draft is gonna be on soon," Bit told Ronnie. His body filled the doorway.

"You turned to it?" he asked. Panic sat just at the corners of his lips.

"No."

"Bit, why didn't you turn to it?" He moved past her and raced down the stairs without an answer.

Ronnie said he remembered seeing Len Bias around, shooting hoops in Maryland before he even went to College Park. "Where?" Bit asked him, but he couldn't give specifics, street names or even cities in Maryland. Was it Landover? Was it Hyattsville? Was it Suitland? "The point is," he would say, waving his hands at all the questions Bit had, "he was here, right here just like us." Bit couldn't imagine anyone better than Janet Jackson, anything better than any of her dance moves or the songs on *Control*, but Ronnie would get angry if she said that. He'd stand up and say they were different. Janet danced on the ground, but Len, he could get up there, be airborne. And this is when Ronnie's arms would grow, take flight away from the sides of his lanky frame, away from their position hanging down by his knees like when he sat on the couch with Dad. This is when he would seem even larger than their father to Bit, and she knew that one day he would be.

Bit followed Ronnie downstairs and into the living room, the color television in a corner where Ronnie and Dad could see it. Bit would sit on the other side of the dining table where she had to lean forward to watch. Her shirts always hovered just above destruction by a plate of food. All she usually missed was the news. As long as Bit cleared the dishes by eight o'clock, she could lie on the floor of the living room and watch all her favorite sitcoms.

Ronnie turned the television to the draft and fiddled with the rabbit ears until the picture came in clearer.

"Hold this," he told her. Bit took the long, metal tuner in her hand. "Stop, stop, stop," he said, pressing his palm to the air as though he were playing a handclap game, like he used to with Bit when she was younger.

They all came to the table. Ronnie was already in his chair and paying attention only to the television. Their father had changed, his clothing and his mouth looser. Callie placed the platter of pork chops closest to him. She had taken the platter out of Bit's hand on the way to the dining room.

"He's gonna go number one, Mr. Sayers?" Callie asked. Bit's mother had herded Callie over to another seat, a seat not on either side of Dad.

"Well, we'll see in a minute, but the number doesn't matter as much as what he does after. That's what matters," he said. He slapped Ronnie's back.

"You're so right," Callie said. She nodded. Bit elbowed her to get her to stop, convinced she was making fun of Bit's father, but there was sincerity in Callie's face.

"What time is your mother coming to get you?" Bit's mother asked Callie. "Or did you call your father?"

Callie stopped her reach for the bowl of potatoes. Bit's mother wasn't mean, but her grip, even when she was reaching out a hand to help you, could be too tight. "Not yet," Callie said.

Ronnie hushed them all as Bias walked up to the podium with a green Celtics cap on. They showed a tape of him dunking, moving from one end of the court to the other in what looked like three steps.

"Look at his reach, Dad," Ronnie said. He moved out of his chair as if he could keep walking right onto the stage and up to Bias.

"But what did he say? He's got potential he hasn't tapped yet. He needs to improve his skills," Dad said. He shook a fork in Bias's direction.

"He's going to sit on the bench though," Ronnie said. He moved away from his seat and got closer to the television. He touched the rabbit ears, but the picture was coming in fine. Ronnie just stood and stared at Bias.

"He won't, not really. But he knows he ain't ready yet," her father said. "He'll get there though." He moved his chair back from the table. "You hear that, Son? Time goes." Dad repeated, "You hear what Red Auerbach said? Time goes."

Ronnie nodded like he was listening, but he wouldn't turn from the screen so Bit could tell if he really was.

* * *

Callie's fingertips traced circles on the dark green phone in the upstairs hallway. She was only pretending to call her mother. She had thanked Bit's mother for the meal and then told Bit's father she hadn't meant to stay this late—*The A-Team* was over—but that she always liked being at their house. "Anytime," he'd said. "We like having you over here." Callie had smiled at this and asked, "Anytime?" "Of course," her father said, "of course." Her mother had left the living room and started washing dishes.

"If my mom finds out you didn't call," Bit warned. Callie waved Bit's worry away. She left Callie at the phone with her make-believe.

In the kitchen, Ronnie was washing dishes. Bit could hear her mother laughing in the other room. Her noise eased into the melody of Anita Baker's "Sweet Love" playing in the living room.

"I'll dry and put away," Bit said. Ronnie turned, his elbows covered in white suds. She picked up a plate and wiped its surface clean of droplets with a dish towel.

"Your little friend still here?" Ronnie said.

"Quit with the *littles*," she said, hitting him in the back with a whip of the towel.

"No way around it, Little Bit," he said.

"We're thirteen now."

"I remember something about that. Something about an important birthday." He made talking motions with one soapy hand and then used it to try and eat Bit's arm.

"Get off. You're getting me all wet."

"You gotta shower sometime, Little Sister."

"Quit it," Bit yelled, but she started to laugh when Ronnie poked a finger in her side. He relented and slid his fingers back into the soapy water. Bit picked up another plate and dried the dish in silence. Callie must still be playing on the phone. If Derrick called, he would get a busy signal.

"How do you know if a boy really likes you?" she asked.

Ronnie took both hands out of the dishwater and turned to face Bit. He grabbed the towel from her hands and wiped the soap off his own.

"What're you talking about?"

"There's a boy," Bit said. She picked up a glass and put it away in the cabinets.

"You like him? You've talked to him?" Ronnie asked. He poked her again in the side. Bit swatted at his hand.

"Kind of."

"Oh okay. And you want to hang out, but you don't know if he wants to hang out?" Ronnie made wide arcs with his index finger from one point to another, creating the distance between her and Derrick.

"I guess. But he didn't call and maybe it's because of what you said."

"That you're a lazy little sister who doesn't help with the dishes?" he asked.

"Ronnie," she whined. "That I'm little, you know, like, still so young."

Ronnie grew still. He turned to the entryway of the kitchen, the one their parents might appear in.

"Don't ever be in a rush to grow up, Bit. There's a lot of good things about being as young as you are, about not having to make decisions about the life you want to live. They make those decisions right now," he said, and pointed toward the living room. "That's okay for now.

It's probably even good for you. But, later, when you get older you start realizing that you gotta make your own choices, you know? It's hard. Harder than you think it is. Bias, you know, people were saying he should be at a place where he can be a star. You know, like be a star right away, on his own. He wouldn't ride any bench or have to wait his turn. You know, he could go and be the thing that people, other people, want him to be. But he said no, there's something more in me and there's something I wanna do that nobody sees coming and I'm gonna go do this thing. I can do this thing. You know? And sometimes that's what being grown is. Knowing who you are, who you really are, even when no one else does."

The words exhausted Ronnie. He turned back to the dishwater and rested his hands on the edges of the sink. Bit didn't know what it was to be almost old enough to leave home and make your own choices, but she did know she longed for the hours she used to play Barbies. The story lines she had created for her dolls played out as she directed. If she changed her mind about an ending, she started again.

"So, what's this boy's name?"

"It's Derrick. Your friend, Derrick."

Ronnie turned back around, the exhaustion gone. "Don't date him."

"He's your friend. Your ace, he said." Bit gathered the memories of the other night to make sure she was saying it just as Derrick had.

"He's not my ace. Don't date him. Don't even like

him," he said. Ronnie still faced her, but his eyes were bricked-over windows. "Liking him is real dumb. It's really fucking dumb." Ronnie turned away from Bit. She didn't hear Ronnie curse much. He did it with other boys, when the beginnings and endings of his words ran out like too much juice in a glass too small. Ronnie's words to her weren't usually ones that needed to be wiped away.

"Don't call me that," she said.

"Then don't be that," he said.

Bit dropped the dish towel on the wet dishes and waited for Ronnie to say he was sorry. He had this slow way of turning his head, looking down and then to the side when he knew he was wrong. She waited for it. A space hollowed out in her chest the longer she waited, the longer he didn't face her. Then she walked out of the kitchen. At the top of the stairs, Callie was holding the phone in her hand and staring at the rotary numbers.

"I'm tired," Bit said. She walked past Callie into her bedroom. She took off her clothes and pulled her nightshirt over her head. Callie followed her, but Bit didn't care if she stayed or went home now.

"I told your mom that my mom didn't answer," Callie said.

"Okay." Bit got into bed and turned away from Callie and toward the window. She heard the unzipping of Callie's jeans, the creak of the floor when she finally lay down.

"Bit?" she asked. The sound was small; Bit would have mistaken it for a yawn or the noise of a nighttime adjustment, fidgeting with a pillow or pulling a blanket up to cover a chilled neck. Usually their sleepovers were too loud for the quiet of night. They wouldn't have been able to stop talking. Bit remained fixed on the outside, listening for a soft knock on her door, a timid advance to an apology from her brother. "Is he ever coming back?"

"I don't know," Bit said.

***

It was the second-to-last day of school. Teachers gazed out the same windows as students waiting for the last bell and handed out crosswords until then. Bit and Callie didn't write any notes to each other, didn't press tattered triangles of notebook paper into each other's hands. Bit didn't feel like putting hearts above *i*'s and looping the ends of *y*'s today.

On the walk to the Metro after school, they saw Derrick, but he didn't come up to them, barely nodded at Bit. He did smile, but Bit was sure it was as much for Callie as it was for her. Ronnie didn't have to worry; Derrick didn't even like her. Callie stopped before the escalators down to the Metro, worried, she said, that she had left things in her locker. Important things. She told Bit to go ahead, that she wasn't going to come over tonight anyway.

"Your mom will kill me if I show up again," she said, walking backward toward the high school.

Bit was glad for the ride home by herself.

It was only a few days after the party, too soon and

expensive for another trip to the Wharf for crabs. But her father walked in that night, just past six, with a large paper bag, Old Bay streaked on the back of it, wetness breaking through the bottom.

"Crabs," he said to Mom. Her face cracked in confusion and joy. "Got them steamed. They're still hot. Get the newspapers, Bit." Ronnie grabbed sodas and put beer in the freezer, and her mother found the leftover potato salad. Her father plugged in the backyard lights. They sat down to dinner. Ronnie was relaxed, the uprightness of his back from the party gone. Bit's insides still churned from their fight, but at least the Ronnie she had wanted to see for weeks was sitting right next to her.

"This year's family reunion, we're gonna have some pictures to show from your graduation," her father said. He drained his second beer and opened a new one.

"You'll get to see California again," Mom said. "You remember it, Ronnie? San Francisco and all that fog?" She put a hand to his face and when he smiled her hand rose with his cheek.

"Yeah. I remember I wanted to wear shorts. You'd only let me bring one pair. I didn't know it would be cold in the summer." Ronnie and Mom laughed together.

"But you loved it. Even if you had to wear jeans most of the time. You loved it."

"And I'll get to go this time," Bit said.

"You were still so young last time," her mother said in consolation.

"You'll love it," Ronnie said to Bit. It wasn't an apology, but Bit would take it. "It felt like the first time I'd been anywhere."

"What do you mean?" Dad asked. "We took you lots of places. Down to North Carolina. Over to West Virginia. You'd even seen Boston by then. That was one of the first trips. You liked Boston. Remember? Maybe you had something to do with Bias going to the Celtics. Two area boys in Beantown. Maybe you'll live there or New York or something. One of the bigger cities after you graduate from Howard." Bit nodded and agreed with her father. No one else did. Ronnie went back to his crab. Her mother slipped her hand away from Ronnie.

"Why was it like the first time you'd been anywhere?" Bit asked. She said it kind of soft, like when Callie had called out her name last night. She wanted Ronnie to hear and answer her, but she wished her father had gone back inside for a minute, that he wouldn't think she was ignoring him.

"I just remember thinking there was so much in the world," Ronnie said. He smiled at Bit, but the joy that should have been on his lips was trapped, maybe sitting on his tongue.

"So much what?" Bit was greedy when it came to Ronnie, stuffing herself full with what he said and did. She never got sick from all that feasting. The hunger was bottomless.

Ronnie shrugged. He started talking when Mom smiled at him. "You just start thinking, all these people, you know, in California or like South America or something, they know all these things I've never even thought of. Like, all these things I didn't even know could be known. I mean, I didn't know that summers aren't all warm in California. There's books. But, I don't know. No pages could tell me what mist would feel like on my legs."

"You'll learn all kinds of things in college," Dad said. "You just wait."

"Ron," Mom said. The beginning of his name shook like she couldn't get the letters to stand up straight. Bit wanted to say it too, to stop her Dad from college talk, right when they were having such a good time. Bit cut her finger on a crab claw. She sucked on it, but the Old Bay was already in there and stung.

"I'm just saying he's got a lot to look forward to," Dad said. "He knows that I'm just getting him excited about what's to come."

"Bias's dad was talking about how bright his future is," Ronnie said.

"A dad can't help but be proud of what his son's about to accomplish. Bias got basketball to succeed in, you could have engineering or architecture or business. One day, Son, maybe you'll be on some big press conference. The whole world talking about what you did." Dad took a swig of his beer. He set it back down too fast and it tipped. Bit couldn't tell if the glow on his cheeks was from the beer or from talking about Ronnie, but his electricity felt larger than when he first came home. Sparks were flying off him and Bit didn't know whether to dance under them or run. "I tell the guys down at the job all about you. I'm always telling them all about you. 'My son,' I say. 'My son.' They make fun of me sometimes, 'You know when Ron's chest gets puffed out it's because he's getting his lungs ready to say, *My son.*' And they're right. You don't know how proud I am of what you're about to do." Her father loved Bit. She never believed anything else, but she already knew her father could never love her the way he loved Ronnie.

"Ron, baby," Mom said. She laughed. "You're starting to ramble. Since when do three beers send you spinning?" She grabbed at his abandoned beer bottle, but it was drained. "Go get more crabs, Ronnie."

Ronnie started to stand, but Dad waved him back down to his seat. Ronnie's face slipped even further from joy.

"I just want you to know that college is gonna be so important. Everything that's about to happen for you is so important," her father said.

"What if what I wanted to do . . ." Ronnie began. "What if what I wanted to do was go away somewhere?" he said. He raised his head at the end of the sentence to face their mother. Their father's face changed. Ropes formed on the sides of his neck, pulling on his brow and closing it into a fist. Bit knew this face, the one before he spanked her when she was younger.

"Why would you do that? You nervous about next year or something?" Dad said.

"No," Ronnie said. He didn't explain, and this silence would only make Dad madder. They were all accountable to him, but Ronnie most of all.

"A man has doubts sometimes, but you face those down."

"It's not doubts."

"I worked. Hard. For you to be able to go to college. Your mother, too," he said. He glanced over and in her face he must have seen, like Bit saw, that she understood something the two of them did not. "Why are you bringing this up tonight?" her father asked. His eyes stayed on their mother. Bit turned to Ronnie. In the kitchen last night, Ronnie had been trying to tell her something she hadn't understood.

"I worked so you would have this tuition, so that you would finish college on time and go live the life you're supposed to live," her father said. He finally turned to Ronnie when he said this, his voice growing louder the longer he spoke.

"I could go see the world and then come back," Ronnie said. His arms rose like when he'd told Bit about where Bias played ball, and now she understood that the places in those stories didn't matter. Ronnie was trying to get off the ground.

"Go see the world? I worked to take care of my family."

"But I can do it on my own. In the time I want. I don't know about college. I know I don't want to stay in DC. Maybe I'll end up in college, maybe I won't. But I know I can't stay here." Bit couldn't understand why Ronnie wanted to leave them, to desert their foursome.

"You're a child. You don't know what you need. You don't know what you want." Dad shook his head at Ronnie and threw his hands to the sky.

"Ron, you should listen to him," her mother said. Bit grabbed for Ronnie's hand, but she didn't manage to hold it in her grasp.

"Now I'm a child?" Ronnie asked. He rose this time. Neither Bit's hand nor her hopes for this summer could have kept him in his seat. "All senior year, you kept telling me I'm a man. I'm a man, you say, but only if I go to college, only if I don't leave like you did before I can get a degree." They never talked back to Dad like that. Their father wasn't a man who gave them beatings, not even when they were kids, spankings were the most severe physical punishment, but Bit readied herself for violence. Bit wanted to hit Ronnie herself for ruining the whole night, the whole summer. He didn't want to be here with them now or later. He would run away to California or wherever else, give up college, make Dad hate him and Mom cry, all because he was too selfish to do anything else.

"Don't get your back too straight, Son. You think you want to go out into those streets. But black men go out and don't come back. You know that?" Dad asked. Ronnie glanced out into the alley, seeing something the same way he had the night of the party. Bit didn't turn this time. She hadn't been able to see what he saw for weeks.

"I'm not them. I'm not you either," Ronnie said.

Her father stood up from his chair, it toppled from the force. "Who are you?" he asked. "Who are you?"

"I'm trying to be me. Whoever that's gonna be."

"Then you should go do that in somebody else's house," Dad said.

"Ron. Now stop it," her mother said. She rose too. Bit stayed seated, grabbed again for Ronnie's hand to get him to sit back down. "Ronnie just needs to talk through this." Even her mother, made of back rubs and whispered words, could not change the course of this night.

"I don't have to talk about anything. I did it. It's done," Ronnie said. "I'm not going to Howard."

Dad slammed his fist into the teak table. The remains of the night, the shells, the discarded bits, clattered and collapsed on each other.

★★★

If Bit had slept, dreams could have rescued her, late-night visions to cure the day's disease. The moon was a single flashlight beam lighting the backyard on its way to Bit's bedroom, illuminating even the crevices. Her father had gone for a drive and Ronnie went to his room, a slammed door and then Run DMC. He was probably asleep, but his music still played even in the middle of the night. Their mother never told him to turn it down.

"He'll be okay?" Bit had asked her mother while they cleared the newspapers and took out the trash themselves.

"Of course," her mother answered. Bit never said which *he*, and her mother didn't either. The whole world was coming apart. No one, not even Ronnie, could have told her, in soothing whispers, "It's fine, everything is just fine."

Bit pressed her nose to the window, breathing out until a fog grew on the glass. She traced her initials and then Derrick's, leaving behind beads of moisture. She didn't understand Ronnie or her father. She didn't understand Derrick either. Her father loved Ronnie but wanted to hurt him. Ronnie loved her but he would move away. Derrick seemed to like her but wouldn't call. Her circle of breath began to fade.

But then Bit's eyes adjusted to the dark, and she saw Ronnie in the backyard, sitting on the teak table all alone. Bit was too scared to go outside in the middle of the night even though she wanted to talk to him. The back bushes stirred and Bit tapped on the window to alert Ronnie, but he wouldn't have heard her from her second-floor window. A boy vaulted over the back foliage that her father had trimmed for the party. He landed on the grass with grace and dusted himself off. Bit couldn't see his face. Ronnie jumped off the table and walked toward him. Both extended their hands, but the boy dropped something on the ground. He picked it up and when he did, the moon pushed away the shadows and Bit could see that it was Derrick. He thumbed through the contents in his hands, counting it. He finally handed it to Ronnie. They nodded at each other as if only passing on the street and Derrick climbed back over the bushes. Ronnie stuffed the bills in his pocket, not bothering to fold or smooth them out, like the bills Derrick had pulled from his pocket the day before. She had seen Derrick smoke weed, the smell of him foreign and pungent when she first met him. Some boys did that, but Ronnie wasn't one of them. He had never smelled that way, never had their sleepy look.

Ronnie hadn't bought anything from Derrick. He hadn't slipped one of those cigarettes behind his ear. Derrick was bringing him money. Ronnie stepped, lithe and quick, toward the back door of the house. Bit pressed her nose back to the window, breathed out, and with the palm of her hand rubbed away the initials.

★★★

In the morning, Bit woke, free at first of the jagged line between what she'd seen last night in the backyard and her dreams. It was the last day of school. In the hours she had to wait for summer vacation to begin, she could figure out what to say to Ronnie. She wanted to tell someone, but she didn't know what she would say: "My brother might be a drug dealer"?

Callie was the holder of Bit's understanding of the world, but Callie hadn't called her last night. Bit couldn't remember when that had ever happened.

Everything was different.

Bit clambered into the morning as she did any other, but the previous night lingered. In the kitchen, her parents readied for work, making breakfast to hold them over until lunch. Ronnie came down the stairs and went to the refrigerator.

"You want food?" Mom asked. Ronnie shook his head. He grabbed the orange juice. He left the door ajar. Their father closed it.

"You gonna get a glass?" he asked. Ronnie opened a cabinet and got a large plastic cup. They both wanted to continue their fight but were slow to throw punches.

"It's my last day of school," Bit announced, the voice of the referee. Her mother smiled at her. Her face was splashed with relief.

"You want some orange juice?" Ronnie asked. Bit only nodded. She wanted him to know she had seen him in the backyard, but she couldn't say that now. She didn't know when she would say it.

Her father turned on the television, a small black-and-white set in a corner. The tube took time to warm up. When the picture came in, the images were scrambled as if they couldn't figure out the right order. On the screen was Len Bias with a Celtics cap on. It was a picture from the draft, right after he'd been picked. Bit remembered his suit had been white and pinstriped, like no suit she'd ever seen. Then, there was a picture of him from University of Maryland, his arms outstretched with biceps snaking from his shoulder to his elbow. A basketball was in each of his large hands. His Celtics jersey flashed on the screen, the green and white in shades of only gray. Under it was type in block letters: LEN BIAS DEAD AT 22.

He had been celebrating, the newscaster told them, driving around town in his newly leased sports car. He met up with some friends. They'd eaten crabs together. He'd gone to another party. Later back at his dorm, Len sat down on a couch. He was talking to a friend. He laid his head back as if he were going to fall asleep, maybe just taking a nap after those long days, and his body started convulsing. He had a seizure. The ambulance came, but he never opened his eyes again. "A heart attack at twenty-two," the newscaster said.

Bit had gone to her first funeral last year: her great-great uncle. She hadn't known him, a branch too high on a vast tree. Her mother asked if she wanted to stay seated when they went up to view the body, but Bit had wanted to see. She couldn't remember him alive, so seeing him dead made no difference. Either way, he wasn't real. He looked plastic, like a life-size doll, and Bit wished she had confirmed it by touching his face. She tried to picture Bias like that, not in motion, not smiling after a win. She had never met him either, but Bias had been real. It was a life needlessly short, like coming inside hours before the streetlights had come on, missing out on the long stretches of sunlight still left.

She reached out and pulled at Ronnie's T-shirt, pulled and pulled. Bit had tried to get Ronnie to smile at the party and now, Ronnie started to cry. He didn't cry like Bit would have, eyes so full of water, a sink overflowing and the faucet still turned on full blast. Instead, Ronnie held on to his bottom lip with his teeth, as if he could have ripped it off.

"Don't you see?" Dad asked.

Ronnie nodded, listening to their father as he had the night of the draft, but this morning he turned away from the television.

No one could box up sorrow as large as Ronnie's over Bias. Bit tried to figure it out all day at school, the last day. Bias was all the boys could talk about, and she saw in them the tremors of their own defeat. Callie didn't come to any of their classes. Bit sat through three movies by herself. The girls around her scribbled notes to each other during the Oompa Loompa songs in *Willy Wonka & the Chocolate Factory*. Bit expected every noise the other kids made during *Jaws* to be Callie opening the wooden doors to the room.

At the end of the day, Bit dropped the contents of her locker into her book bag. She took down her pictures of Janet, New Edition, and Wham! Maybe she would hang them in her locker next year or maybe she would care too much about new things to hold on to all that she used to love. Bit searched for Callie, but as the school emptied, she wasn't in any of the echoing halls.

She slowed her walk past the high school, unable to stop herself from hoping to see Derrick. And she saw him. Him and Callie. She fingered the bottom of Derrick's polo. He pulled on one of her curls and watched it bounce. Callie was in cutoff shorts and a tank top. She looked tan. She had been in the sun, probably in her backyard. Her father had hung a hammock from two of their trees last summer. Callie had lazed in the grass near her father in a spot where the trees parted to let in the sun. She must have lain there all yesterday and today because her calves and thighs were golden and those limbs, crossed and dangling off the edge of the concrete block Derrick stood in front of, were perfect. Her curls were tucked behind her ear. Callie closed her eyes and pressed her lips together and out. All of her, the perfect thighs and the coils of her hair and her lips, glossed and pursed, moved toward Derrick.

★★★

When Bit got to the Red Line stop, she stood on the platform that took her farther away from her home. She took the train to the end of the line, got off, and rode the other way. She passed up her stop that time and three times after. A little girl would have cried, but if you were thirteen, if you were almost grown, you weren't supposed to cry.

When she finally got home, her mother met her at the door.

"Why are you just getting in?"

"I was at Callie's," Bit said. The lie came out fast and fluid. Ronnie had been lying. Callie definitely had been lying and betraying. Her father didn't want to hear the truth. Growing older meant hiding things from people and Bit felt more mature today than she ever had.

"So you haven't seen Ronnie?" Her mother's voice was sometimes a tool of torture. The shouts when Bit hadn't washed the dishes, the low-voiced threats when Ronnie and Bit wouldn't stop messing with each other. Her voice now was a different kind of torture, the strangle of a helplessness Bit hadn't known her mother capable of.

"No," Bit said. She didn't want to see her mother upset and Bit didn't want to cry either. She went upstairs instead to lie in bed until the evening made way for night. Her mother never came upstairs to ask her anything more. Bit turned on her side, and out of her window, the one that had betrayed her the night before, she was relieved to find Ronnie in the backyard. His shoulders hunched over the teak table. The points of him began to shake and Bit knew that he was crying, harder than he had that morning. Then he straightened and his thin frame became larger, more massive.

It was her father.

She dozed off and woke at the creak of the steps, an exclamation Bit didn't ignore. She got out of bed and peered out of her bedroom door. Ronnie's was ajar. He must have come home. She put her jeans back on and slipped her feet into her house shoes. By the time she got to the front door, Ronnie was already down the block in shorts and gym shoes. She would have run after him, to grab him by his arm even if he only pulled it away, but she couldn't run in her slippers.

Bit was afraid of night in DC, the news so insistent about how bad crime was. The world menaced, the newscasters said. Terrors in the streets, when Bit used to worry more about monsters in closets and creatures under beds. "Shhh, there's nothing to worry about," her father used to tell her. "Bit, it's fine, it's fine," Ronnie had said.

She followed Ronnie to the basketball court at the nearby junior high and there he was shooting baskets like he was playing Bias. Faking, stealing, flexing his calves, stretching his arms to sink the ball. Bit didn't go onto the court. She stayed on the other side of the chain-link fence, too afraid to violate whatever peace he was making under the watch of the hoop. She laced her fingers through the holes of the fence and shook it, the groan of the slumbering metal echoing in the dark. Harder, she pushed and pulled the barrier between her and Ronnie.

She couldn't stay here forever.

Her mother might have heard the door closing twice. Her father might have gone inside and wondered why she wasn't in bed. She would need to get back home, but she could frame Ronnie in one diamond of this fence, frame his reaching, and have something of him all her own to keep. His hands were raised high, as if he could tug on the moon and have the whole world come hurtling toward him. All that love and trouble, as wide and long as the sky.

FINAL DRAFT OF COLLEGE ESSAY

Dear Sirs and Madams:

Maybe I don't need to be that formal, but this is my essay for entrance into your university. Your question asked only for me to tell you something about myself and so that is what I have set forth to do upon this space given in the online application. I know that this is my real shot to get into your school. You will look at my grades and my SAT scores, which I think you will find suitable, but perhaps not stellar. So, I hope then that in these paragraphs I will show you something about myself that will make you want me.

Firstly, I live in Washington, DC, the capital of our nation, the seat of democracy for all these United States. As a result—foremost, or as previously mentioned, firstly—I could be considered a student of history. Who could not walk among the marbled buildings of this wide-avenued city and not be? In my opinion, no one could. My parents would take me down to the Lincoln Memorial sometimes, and there my dad would say, "Look! The emancipator of our people." I would look and look some more at the large seated figure of one Abraham Lincoln. Right there, even as a small child, I was witness to the greatness of the past. I come by this curiosity naturally as both of my parents are inquisitive people. They ask a lot about my life and that's how I know that they are very inquisitive people.

When they tortured people and asked them a lot of things about what they thought about stuff in Spain, it was called the Spanish Inquisition. This is similar to what my parents do. They do it because they love me and it is nice at least to be the beneficiary of such warm and tender feelings. They do not, however, love my sister in this same smothering way. Perhaps this is too personal, but I think you should know all of this. She does not like to watch *Nova* on PBS like I do; instead she goes out frequently rather than sporadically as I do. When I do not leave the house, they ask me why I have not left the house. When I do leave the house, they ask me where I am going. My mother will ask with a large grin on her face, while she rubs my back and wonders what friend I will be meeting at my destination that Saturday. She does not know that I am rarely, or more precisely never, meeting anyone. Thereby, leading me to my second point.

Secondly, I am alone a lot. I think this makes me a more introspective and thoughtful person. I am an independent thinker because I do not have a crew of friends who try to get me to think the way they think. I did have friends when I first started high school, but we are no longer close. They started making out with boys on the backs of buses and going to parties where people were drinking and smoking. I was curious (as I said that is natural to me), but one boy in particular (whose name I will withhold here) with whom I could have shared an intimate moment did not want to share one with me. He made an uncouth noise such as *ewww* or *hell no*, I think, and then he laughed. My "friends" only laughed along with him and said later, when I was in tears with my legs tucked into my chest and my head on my knees just under the large magnolia tree in the backyard of the house on Irving Street, that I should stop crying like a baby. "Did I want to be a nerd all my life?" they asked. I didn't answer them because I don't think I'm a nerd and I had cried so much that my nose had gotten stuffed up and I could not breathe and I did not have any tissues. I still tried to hang out with them, but I couldn't put eyeliner on like they could and I got tired of them and their new friends telling me things only to say *sike* after it. They might say, "That is a cute outfit Kara," and then say, "Sike!" as in negating the very thing that they had said previously.

The very end of our association, however, came when they began telling me that there was somebody in the school who didn't like me and who thought that I said stupid things. They promised that they would help me figure out who the person was and beat the person up if necessary. My "friends" and their new "friends" started giving me a clue each day over the course of a week.

I guessed every day. I went to my classes trying to figure out who it could be and whispering guesses to my "friends." Finally, they told me, "Kara, don't you get it. The person who doesn't like you is in your classes, lives near you, went to your junior high school, and hangs out with a cool crowd." I still could not guess and I looked at my two best "friends" for them to tell me who it was. Maybe they would tell me that they did not want to be with their new crew anymore, but wanted it to be the three of us again like it had been since elementary school. They did not tell me. They laughed. All of them started to laugh and said, "It's us." My best "friends" were referring, if that was not clear in the retelling, to themselves. They had, in cahoots with these new people, conspired against me and therefore betrayed any trust that remained in me. I thought that we knew and understood each other, these young women and I. Little was I privy to the knowledge that they in fact no longer wanted to have anything in common with me. I had not fully, until that very moment, realized that years of friendship meant nothing to those girls. That I thought we were the same kind of people leads me to my last point before my conclusion.

Thirdly, I am my own kind of black girl. However, I do not know if I am the kind that you will want or not. I do not always get my hair done. I do not like going to the beauty salon where the hairdresser will complain that my hair is so thin I should think about getting extensions put in. I do not listen to hip hop, except for the very occasional fun rapper such as Macklemore or, when I'm feeling old-school, Coolio. I would rather listen to singer-songwriters from the 1960s and 1970s. Most young adults my age would not know the people whose albums I have wholeheartedly embraced. They should know about Carole King, I feel, but they may never. Everyone should listen to "So Far Away" or "You've Got a Friend." I am not the kind of black girl who is meant to be in high school. I am the kind of black girl who should be in college. I know that there is much to my mind, but I have been unable to access all those parts of it in this environment. I assumed that high school was going to be a certain type of thing. "Some of the best years of my life" is what my father once said. I have not found that to be true. I think there must be, though in the larger, wider world, girls who are like me. They may be quieter or less conventional and they may not yet be very appealing to the opposite sex, but they are good-hearted, real people who would not intentionally hurt anyone else or call them a baby if they found another person crying under a tree with bits of pollen stuck in her hair.

In conclusion, I believe that I should be granted entrance into your school. I wrote this essay myself without benefit of the aid of my parents (as I mentioned they are very busy) and without the aid of a tutor. I read in the *Washington Post* (a publication I read often and voraciously) that some students and their parents pay for someone to either write or cowrite these kinds of essays to ensure that they will get into their first choice. I have not done that. Although if my parents had the money, I don't know that I wouldn't. It would be a nominal fee to pay for the privilege of having the life you want, as that is not what I have right now, at this time. I am applying only to this school because I truly believe that I will find what I am looking for in the halls of your esteemed university. If you allow me to matriculate at your institution, I think that you will not regret that wise decision. I think it is important to feel chosen, and I am choosing you.

I hope you will choose me, too.

With all sincere and due respect,
Kara N. Tompkins

PART TWO
The Upper School

THE ROPES

Fifth graders were savages. Cannibals really, devourers of each other and of Dawn. If that had been in the Watson Elementary School handbook ("III. Beware the fifth-grade savage.") instead of fire-code violations and summer-vacation dates, Dawn might never have taken this job. She liked kids, but she didn't know about *these* kids.

And the new girl, Clarissa, was their afternoon snack.

She introduced herself, layered in ruffles and ribbons, without twisting the tips of her dark red leather shoes into the floor or fidgeting with the hem of her patterned dress. Instead, she stood still with her light brown arms out, as if paused midtwirl.

"Your name is Old Lady," Ebony, the tall and awkward girl in the last row, said.

"Do not speak out of turn," Dawn scolded. Ebony was Queen of the Cannibals. Dawn leaned harder into the bulletin board, where she had stapled paper letters that spelled out TODAY IS A NEW DAY FILLED WITH PROMISE. She bought supplies for her room whenever she could, brighter colored paper, larger stencils, anything to get their attention.

Jamel and Anthony, cutting up as usual, started making noises. Clarissa paused for them to finish and began from where she had started. She said her own name with reverence. Cla-ris-sa. No one interrupted the second time, but their sour faces said enough.

Cannibals ate the best meat first.

"We welcome Clarissa to our class, don't we?" Dawn said. She smiled at the girl, and though the edges of Dawn's mouth barely lifted most days, she lugged her cheeks away from her chin up to very near her eyeliner to give a real smile. "You can have a seat, Clarissa."

Clarissa moved away from the front of Dawn's desk and back to the metal desk she'd been placed in alphabetically. Two months into the school year, Dawn knew all thirty-two names without relying on the seating or attendance sheet.

"Who has their homework? So we can show Clarissa what we've been learning," Dawn said. The heels of her sensible and ugly teacher shoes percussed her to the front of the room.

Ebony raised her hand first. Her fingertips were as permanent a fixture in the room as the fluorescent lights lining the cracked ceiling. Her buzz, too, just as constant. Dawn called her forward. Ebony dragged her limbs and Dawn's classroom time behind her. She took a pencil off a boy's desk, only for him to shout "Hey!" long after it was between her teeth. Dawn forced a smile and ignored the thievery.

"Ebony, if you were running for mayor of DC, what would your slogan be?" Dawn joined her fingers in front of her so she wouldn't rub her temples, the place headaches started with this girl.

Ebony gathered herself for the oratory. She stretched her arms so that the wrinkled piece of notebook paper was parallel to the self-satisfied expression on her face.

"My slogan is 'Because I said so.'" Ebony smiled and dropped her arms. The notebook paper fluttered to the ground and Ebony bowed. Her slogan could have been "Trouble first." Simple, truthful, to the point.

"What do we think of her slogan, class?" Dawn asked. She layered encouragement over her irritation, soaking up the Potomac with a wad of paper towels. The children shook their heads no and those who had started to slowly nod yes reversed course at the sight of Dawn's crossed arms and the tap of her foot. "What do we need for a great slogan, class?"

From far corners of the room, she heard the words she had written on the board a couple of days ago: *Action. Optimism. Brevity.*

"Do we think Ebony's slogan encompassed action, optimism, and brevity?" No one answered. Her voice had lost the screech of authority and the children weren't sure what answer would keep them out of trouble. "Class, did she?" She walked toward the blackboard behind her desk and away from Ebony to write the words up again. The chalk scraped at the end of *Optimism*. "Did she?"

Dawn heard her desk creak, and when she turned around, Ebony was pressing a hand at the end of one long, skinned-elbow arm into the oaken surface.

In the front row, Jackie stuck her hand high. She flung her wrist around as if waving off a swarm of gnats, but at least she had finally deciphered the right answer. "No, Mrs. Williams, she didn't."

No matter how many times she told them she wasn't a Mrs., only a Ms., some of them never got it right. Ebony raised her hand again, her fingers reaching out toward Dawn's face, and started speaking with her hand still in the air.

"My mother says it all the time. It inspires me to act by getting up to clean my room because otherwise I'm very optimistic she'll give me a beating." Ebony paused as if on a sitcom and was met with a laugh track. All the classroom was a stage for her.

"Thank you. Have your seat." Dawn waited for Ebony's leisurely processional back to her desk before she spoke again. "Remember our discussion about the slogans of the mayoral race?" Since becoming a teacher, Dawn felt like she asked a lot of questions without the expectation of an answer. "Carol Schwartz is running under the theme of renewal, and she includes in that her five f's: flight, filth, fear, frustration, and financial chaos." The students nodded like they remembered her saying that the day before, but she didn't catch recognition in most of their looks.

She couldn't reveal her unwavering support for Carol Schwartz, but she instructed them in morals and ethics, two things the crack-smoking Marion Barry didn't have. She asked if they thought someone should be trustworthy to run the city. She asked if that person should have a record of lawfulness and responsibility. They nodded. She walked the aisles of the room to give her words weight. Intimidation was her best teaching tool.

Even Dawn had to admit, though, he was running a smart campaign. The new wife, browner than the last, with natural hair closely cropped, was good for the re-election bid. A regular kind of woman, probably someone Barry should have been with all along.

The wife before, Effi, was bejeweled and sunglassed with precisely styled hair. Effi didn't sit on the thin, molding comforter at a hotel while he got his fix. If she were a first lady, Dawn imagined she could be like Effi. Some Washingtonians called Effi cold, but she just wasn't common like her husband, too loud and too prone to mop up his ever-glistening forehead with a rag from his pocket. Effi even sat through his trial with refinement, hooking a rug while witness after witness told stories that wiped their feet on her life. When the FBI and the prison sentence finally came, Dawn was sure Barry would never have power or acceptance again.

But, four years after his arrest, he was trying to run this city again. All that talk he came to Ward 8 with two years ago: he wasn't perfect, but he was perfect for DC. Dawn now would be like Effi then: too good for any of it.

"A slogan lets the voters know what will happen if you get elected. This is important. History is in the making,"

Dawn said. She said this often, to students who didn't turn in their homework or in tandem with threats of the principal's office. "We're going to make our own history." She paused. Teaching was live theater. "Mock election," she singsonged. She waved small slips of paper at them. "The real election is in two days, but we'll have ours today."

Dawn had spent hours on her couch cutting the pieces of paper, first plain white paper, then red and blue construction paper, until finally she found red card stock. Michael wouldn't help with the ballots or the voting booth. This is what she had wanted, she told him, work of significance. He could be at ten thousand feet working at the Department of ED, but she was boots on the ground. She wanted to make an impact. She wanted to be a different kind of teacher to usher in a new era of education! But the glue holding the voting booth's cardboard edges together gave up overnight. She shouldn't have used the school-issued glue stick.

A couple of the boys raised their hands and parroted back what she said about history, then raised their *V*'s for victory. Dawn didn't think any of them knew they were imitating Nixon. Too much American political history would be a waste, but a mock election would win them for the afternoon. She dropped the rectangular pieces of paper onto their desks. They clamored to pick up pencils and pens.

"You'll put a *B* for Barry or an *S*." She coughed a bit on the *S*, so she would have to repeat it. "You'll put an *S* for Schwartz."

Clarissa raised her hand, holding it steadily in the chalk-dusted air. She wasn't a shy girl. Dawn nodded at her.

"Could we say something about the candidates?" Clarissa asked. The other kids rejoiced at being able to make noise, and it would fill the last half an hour before dismissal.

"Who wants to speak on behalf of Barry?" Dawn asked. Ebony raised her hand first, but Dawn scanned the room for someone else. She believed in finding the best person for the task. Anthony had just his palm and wrist in the air. "Anthony for Barry. And for Carol Schwartz?"

The remaining hands went down. No one wanted to speak on behalf of the Republican white lady, but then Clarissa's steady arm raised once again.

"Ms. Williams?" she asked, but Dawn knew it was more like an acknowledgment of an already agreed upon appointment.

"Clarissa." Dawn held her name aloft, as Clarissa had in her introduction. She stood by her desk. Anthony did too, but Dawn let Clarissa go first.

"My father says," she began, "that Barry had his time. He says that Carol Schwartz can do for this city what that man could not. He says that she can bring money into the city and that Barry represents the poorest ward in the city and the poorest, most ignorant people if they vote for him." Dawn thought of her mother and her sister and her childhood home on Minnesota Avenue. Still, Dawn had said as much as Clarissa's father when Barry got elected to the city council.

"Thank you," she told Clarissa, who smoothed and gathered the back of her dress before sitting. She was an elegant little girl. Dawn nodded for Anthony to speak.

"Barry has been doing this a long time," he started. "He has experience." He stood still after, rolling his pencil back and forth on top of his desk. He moved his lips to speak again, but then his jaw slackened, giving up on the words before they began.

Then, Ebony yelled from her seat. "He's from my neighborhood. He represents Southeast. And he's black. He done a lot for this city. My mom say people got jobs because of him. And there weren't as many knuckle-heads out here on these streets shooting each other because Barry gave them summer jobs. And besides, my cousin say we can't have any white lady running this city. This Chocolate City, not White Chocolate City." The other kids laughed and nodded to ideas they were short of information on.

"We don't vote based on race," Dawn told them. They quieted down. "Or on geography." She held gazes around the room. Stern looks were her second-best teaching tool. "Write your votes."

The children set to scribbling on their papers. Some letters were so big that Dawn could see a number of *B*'s even from the front of the room. Others wrote very tiny letters in the corner of their paper rectangles, but they also looked like *B*'s.

She tallied up the letters while they asked who the others voted for, most made *B* motions in the air with their fingers. Excitement wasn't just infectious for these kids, it was a disease that crippled the population with its symptoms of rapid talking and air jabbing. No number of *stay stills* or *stay calms* could cure it. Dawn counted once, and then again. Twenty-two to ten.

Kids didn't know anything.

She laid her palms on the desk. "Barry wins," she announced. The children cheered. Ebony stomped her feet and chanted his name. The other kids followed her as they often did, the stomps rippling over the tile floor. They pounded fists on their rickety desks and raised wiggling fingers high and then higher. The whole classroom seized with cries of his name.

"Elections are serious," Dawn yelled over the chants. She stood up and her chair scraped the floor in agitation. "Democracy is on the move," she reminded them. She thought that slogan up two weeks ago, right before the first bell. Better than "Democracy in action." But today, *move* got them out of their seats just as the bell rang.

"Look, Ms. Williams," Jamel said, ticking and twisting, as she pleaded for them to gather their belongings. "I'm on the move, just like democracy."

***

Dawn preferred when her mother came to their home in Shepherd Park for dinner, but Michael didn't mind driving, and this way her mother couldn't accuse her of being ashamed of Southeast. Except there on the lawn was reason to be, a "Marion Barry '94" sign staked into the small brown lawn of her childhood home.

Dawn waited until after the lemon meringue pie Michael insisted they bring had been sliced to bring it up: "Why do you have a Barry sign?" she asked.

Her mother didn't even like politics.

"His supporters are always walking through the neighborhood," she said. Her mother spread out the "Carol Schwartz for Mayor" pamphlets Dawn brought for her to take to her Bible study. "Nobody wants these. People believe in Barry."

"There's no *u* in his name, Ma," Dawn said. *Burrow*. *Bur-ry*. Like there was something he was hiding. When Dawn started college at George Washington, she worked to rid her voice of the DC accent so no one could ask if she was from the "er-ea," not *area*.

"You embarrassed about your Philly accent, Michael?" Her mother lit up a cigarette and pulled its menthol-flavored smoke into her mouth. She pushed her piece of pie away.

"Can't say I am, Vi." Michael loved for her mother to be on his side, but it wasn't a question he should even answer. Michael's accent wasn't real Philly. He'd been a member of the rich-kids club, Toby & Tiffany, escorted girls from families with five generations of college-educated free Negroes to cotillions, studied from high school through grad school in landscaped New England towns. He didn't disown Philly because it didn't belong to him. Or him to it.

"He smokes crack. He's been to prison. He isn't good

for the city." Dawn tried not to yell, the curtains might complete their unraveling at the timbre of her voice.

"You don't know what he did for this city, LaDawn. He isn't the first black person to get into something he can't get out of. Can't say he'll be the last." She ashed into a supermarket-brand cola can.

"This is the problem. We're always letting people off the hook. It's only November and I've sent Ebony to the principal's office six times already. They probably need to send the girl back to her neighborhood school."

"You stay complaining about that girl."

"Well, I have reason. Principal Anderson told me when she was placed in my class that she might cause trouble."

"You wanted to teach," her mother reminded her.

"Because I like kids," Dawn said. She waited for Michael to defend her, but he remained lapdog loyal to her mother. At least Dawn was rewarded in other people's tender validation of teachers. They were scared of the public school children on the Metro who ate bagged pickles and Hot Fries outside of corner stores. Her courage was rare, so she must be rare. And Dawn would rub between her eyes as if a single, shining unicorn horn were there and say, "It is tough, but it is so very rewarding." Except that feeling was never enough to keep her voice pliant and patient when, for the fourth time, she had to tell her class to stay in a straight line on their way to the auditorium for assembly.

"Then you gotta deal with all them kids. Even this little girl you don't like."

"I never said I didn't like her," Dawn said. "I just wish

she would be better behaved. She's only ten and she's already on a path." Her mother had kept her and her sister in the elementary school nearest their house instead of getting special permission to send her to a better school like Watson. At least Ebony had that going for her, even if she insisted on keeping too much Southeast with her.

"I'm gonna make some tea," her mother said.

"I can do that, Vi." Michael got up and opened and closed battered wooden cabinets.

"She doesn't use a kettle," Dawn said. She stood and reached into a cabinet Michael had already opened to get out a rusted metal pot. The kettle Dawn bought her mother for Christmas three years ago had never been used.

"I told LaDawn that good enough is fine with me. She tries to forget good enough raised her and her sister."

Dawn filled the pot and set it on the old gas stove, pristine from lack of use. Her mother lived on Chinese takeout, cigarettes, and caffeine.

"Shame on me wanting better than good enough. Tanya doesn't even come back to DC." Unlike Dawn, Tanya had escaped DC as soon as she could, all the way to California, and never looked back. Once, on a visit to her sister and her family, someone inquired where in DC they had grown up. Tanya was quick to reply, "Upper Northwest."

"Oh, don't be that way, LaDawn," Michael said. He only used that name to tease. "Our roots are certainly important, Vi." Michael could one day run the Department of ED or be mayor of DC and this was why; he was annoyingly political.

"We're buying a house. In Shepherd Park," Dawn said. This would shift the alliances, she and Michael once again together.

"Time was you married before you moved in," her mother said. "You already living together, don't you think you need that next step? I was married and had you by this time, LaDawn."

"I know, Ma." Her parents had been married for thirty-five years, but only two of those had been spent in the same home. Her mother was pregnant with Tanya when their father moved out. Over the years, Dawn and Tanya received birthday cards and infrequent, short phone calls from their father. He lived in West Virginia with another woman, but her mother's mail was still addressed to Mrs. Viola Williams.

"Don't worry, Vi, your daughter and I have a plan," Michael said. He sat back down across from her mother. Dawn resisted asking him what their plan was.

"DCPS teachers get a break on down-payment costs," Dawn said.

Her mother squinted in reply, but Dawn decided it was only from the smoke.

They left soon after, Michael walking ahead of her to his luxury car. Ma walked Dawn to the door and hand-ed her back a Carol Schwartz button. Dawn crossed the threshold, but her mother pulled on her arm.

"He putting in for this house?" her mother whispered, but Michael was too far to hear.

"Of course, Ma," Dawn said. They had not discussed the financials. Dawn had been so excited by the idea of their signatures together on a piece of paper, she hadn't figured out all the steps they would need to take together.

"Okay." Her mother released her.

Down Minnesota, two boys rode a bike, one on the front wheel with his elbows hooked around the handlebars. They coasted toward the moon.

"Don't get yourself in trouble," Dawn's mother shouted, but Dawn didn't know if she was saying it to her departing back or to the boys.

* * *

Girls liked to play games: double Dutch, hopscotch, handclap, best friend today and enemy tomorrow. It was why girlhood had never suited Dawn. In particular, Dawn had never been good at double Dutch, never mastered the coordination for jumping or turning. The neighborhood girls teased her about it until she gave up on that rite of black girlhood and consoled herself with games of hopscotch with Tanya in front of their house. Some of those girls still lived around her mother's way, the little girls they gave birth to jumping to the rhymes their mothers still hummed in their rented kitchens.

But if she had to supervise recess, Dawn would rather referee girls waiting their turn at the ropes on the blacktop than boys kick-fighting their way through the grassy field.

Today, like most days, Ebony got the rope from the activity room first after she had pulled and bullied it out of another girl's hands. Dawn would be the adult if she had to, reprimanding Ebony by sounding out every syllable of her name Dawn's mouth could get ahold of, but she would rather the other girls who wanted to turn be dejected than have Ebony back in class acting out the rest of the afternoon.

"I'll turn," Ebony declared. She was the best turner in the school after all, which she announced while waving the rope above her head. When Ebony turned, the ropes hit the ground clean, a crisp click-clack not muddled like the turns of girls who were double-handed, a source of shame for any black girl.

The coolest girls, the ones already primed for social domination, praised Ebony for her position as turner and gave the first chance to jump to the little girl Ebony must have snatched on. The rest of the group formed a loose, snaking line for their turn. The littlest girls, those in the second and third grade, were too cowed by admiration for the older ones. They wanted to jump too, their skinny, ashy legs wobbling with anticipation, but they might not get a chance.

The rope hit the blacktop with punitive force. The accumulation of dried fall leaves did not stop the girls from double Dutch. During the winter at indoor recess, they would play inside the cafeteria/auditorium/gym. The stuffy air of that space would not feel like the wind generated by those ropes in the autumn breeze. Girls who got a long turn would become flush and dewy with exertion. They dreamed as they jumped: about the boyfriend's name, about the babies, about the career the chant said they would have. The perfect life that waited for them if they just kept their feet right and stayed off the ropes.

Clarissa stood off to the side of the rope at first. The rope was doubled and Ebony looped the closed end around her waist. Her wrists swung in and out while she leaned forward. One of the cool girls, Jahari, supervised the line of jumpers, nodding to the next girl in line. Jahari was not in Dawn's class, but she was a good girl routinely admired by the teachers. If she were found in the hall during class, no one even asked for her bathroom pass. Jahari moved closer to Clarissa and touched her arm. Dawn stepped forward hoping to witness Jahari slipping an arm through Clarissa's, maybe cupping a hand to her ear to whisper, "I'm gonna tell you a secret." But all Jahari did was elbow Clarissa toward the line of jumpers. Clarissa moved away from the insistence. Her high ponytail reiterated her refusal.

Dawn understood. At faculty meetings, she spoke only when forced. Other teachers with seniority and entitlement, led especially by Mrs. Brown, used their time in the meeting to tell the principal what she wasn't doing right and what they wouldn't be doing to correct it. Dawn answered direct questions. She nodded with vigor to encourage whoever was talking whether she agreed with them or not. She never liked to take her turn, but Clarissa finally did with a little more encouragement from Jahari.

The ropes swung faster as Clarissa approached. Those swift-moving threads dangerous, liable to welt the baby fat of an arm if you timed it wrong. The ropes advanced and then receded and the moment had to be seized when one rope was underfoot and one sailed overhead. Clarissa tried to catch up with Ebony's dance. She could call it wrong and jump directly into the rope or time the jumping in right but not the rhythm. The girls would make fun of her. The ropes hissed through the air. Clarissa paused in her lean. She straightened: her back, her neck, her folded arms. She waited as she had in the classroom for the moment that she was ready. Clarissa was just about to jump. The tension came back into her neck. The skirt of her dress lifted under the poised leap of her thighs. Then, she stepped back, clasping her hands in front of her and watched again. She dropped her hands and took a step back toward the rope. The tension returned to her body and this time she leaned forward, her rear poking out to help her. But when the rope swung close to her face, Clarissa lost her stance. Ebony probably did that on purpose.

"Go already. Damn," Ebony said. Her hands started working overtime to turn. Whatever window Clarissa might've leapt through was gone.

"Ebony," Dawn yelled. "We do not curse and we especially do not curse at people."

"But Ms. Williams, she slow or something?" Ebony lowered the ropes and gestured to the still and straightened Clarissa with her head. Ebony's small braids swayed and covered part of her set jaw.

"Stop it. That's not nice," Dawn said. The other girls hushed themselves. If she raised her voice more, one of the little girls would start using the trouble phrases.

"Oooh, you're in trouble." "Oooh, you're gonna get it." "Oooh, you're gonna be on punishment." She should make Ebony apologize, but Dawn would pay for that later. She had a nice afternoon of silent reading and worksheets planned. Ebony could ruin everything, devour the day's comfort. Dawn turned away from Ebony to take in Clarissa's rounded cheeks. The girl's face flexed.

"She probably doesn't know how to jump. She's up here faking," Ebony said. She dropped the ropes and held her arms aloft above her jeans just like Clarissa did above her dress. Ebony put on a simpering smile and stared out to the crowd of girls with eyes rounded and vacant. A few of Ebony's supporters offered up giggles for her impression.

"No more double Dutch," Dawn said. The group moaned as if they'd all been struck with the rope.

"You can't say that about me." Clarissa's firm voice exceeded Dawn's expectations. She did not stammer or lurch from word to word trying to get the sentence out. Ebony must've heard the strength. She should learn she couldn't just push everybody around.

"Ms. Williams, why you stop the game? I was just playing." Ebony jammed the tip of her white sneaker into the blacktop. She pushed her braids behind one deeply brown ear and Dawn noticed that her face was crooked. One cheek higher than the other, one nostril drooped. Ebony was jealous, mad this little girl was better than her. Dawn almost wanted to crouch down, look her in her face and tell her so. Let her go home and think about that all night.

"You've got twenty minutes left. Go play something else," Dawn said. The girls herded away. Ebony trailed behind doing some sort of dance, a victory one maybe for getting away with her mess. Clarissa remained in her jumping spot, reclasping her hands in front of her. Dawn touched the top of Clarissa's head and the girl looked up to smile at her.

"It's good when we make people do the right thing," Dawn said.

* * *

It was more like ten minutes that they had left to play by the time most of the girls wandered into the grass or wrapped their legs around the brightly colored plastic of the jungle gym. Mr. Espinoza rang a bell on the field and Mrs. Brown rang one on the blacktop. Dawn's kids lined up, their elbows wounding her as she counted them off. She called out "Straight line!" but that didn't do much. "We'll stay here until you're ready to go" only worked for ten seconds before they lost it. She would drop off the other classes in her wing. The easiest was to keep her class at the back and, if she saw mischief, mete out punishment later. Dawn didn't even notice what her class was doing because the third-grade boys were obsessed with a game, shooting fingers and throwing bombs from fists that resulted in the yelling of "You're dead. I killed you." The echoes sounded like gang warfare.

"Watch your girls back there," Mrs. Brown said on her way past Dawn's line. Dawn nodded with confidence. Mrs. Brown was the old guard at the school and definitely a Barry supporter.

Dawn was ready for silent reading, two hours of peace to get to the end of the day. At the doorway of Mrs. Brown's room, Jahari paused before going in and only said to Dawn, "Clarissa got hurt." Dawn nodded and patted the girl on her back. Jahari would get over any trauma from today's double Dutch. There would be other things to worry about between now and 3:15. But two doors down, the students filed in and at the end of the line was a frowning Clarissa and an even more deeply frowning Ebony.

"Both of you stay here," Dawn said. "Silent reading," she commanded the rest of the class.

The girls said nothing, only leaned against the creamy yellow walls of the school. The Thanksgiving decorations were already lining the hallway. Right above the girls was a turkey head, the mouth open and the words *gobble gobble* taped to the beak.

"What happened?" Dawn asked. The girls' eyes were wet. Clarissa's high ponytail was a bit off-center, but for all Dawn could remember right now she might have had a jaunty side hairdo. She had a smear of dirt on her cheek and her arms were at her sides, her coat sleeves covered in dirt, maybe some glitter too. The stuff was everywhere in this school, even far from the art room. Inside her coat, the crisp layers of Clarissa's dress had fallen, but neither that nor the glitter nor the side ponytail mattered when

Dawn saw her knee. Her tights were torn and on her knee was a bright red streak. Dawn crouched.

This time she only asked Clarissa: "What happened?"

"Ebony," Clarissa said. Her large eyes filled. She seemed breakable.

"Ms. Williams." Ebony shook her head. "Ms. Williams." Her eyes also softened, but that was a manipulation. She wasn't pliable and certainly not a kid who would break.

"She did this to you, Clarissa?" Dawn asked. She waited for Ebony to jump in with her protest. Clarissa began a more deliberate cry. "History is in the making, Ebony," Dawn told the girl. Ebony was suddenly smaller, less spindly limbs and more chest. The center of her collapsed and then exploded with the force of her rapid breathing.

"Ms. Williams," Ebony said. "Ms. Williams." The girl rocked back and forth on her feet on the hallway floor until her shoulder blades touched the tile wall. She shook her head no, as if merely loosening up her neck. "Ms. Williams" was all Ebony said as Dawn asked the teacher next door to cover her class and all Ebony kept saying as Dawn took Clarissa to the nurse and walked Ebony to the principal. The chant didn't soften Dawn; she wanted to hear it no more than Ebony chanting Barry's name.

Principal Anderson deemed the situation serious when Dawn described how bloodied Clarissa's leg was. Ebony owned up to nothing.

"Why don't you go sit outside for a minute, Ebony?" Principal Anderson asked. Ebony obeyed, as docile as a tased prisoner.

"I've wanted her inner discipline to finally show itself,

but . . ." Dawn tilted her head and hoped Principal Anderson saw disappointment.

"I knew she would be a challenge. We don't often receive children like her given the neighborhood."

"And a challenge, I think even in my first few months, I was up for, but I think now we see it may be deeper than we thought."

"The girl's home is broken, you know. Single mother, in Northeast, I think."

"Southeast," Dawn corrected by reflex and then wished she had been less accurate.

"Right. Even harder. We'll call her mother to come get her. Clarissa's mother too."

Back in her classroom, Dawn's students asked where Ebony and Clarissa were, but Dawn told them only to mind their reading. Neither the silence nor the whisper of pencils working on vocabulary crosswords quieted the repetition of Ebony's "Ms. Williams" in Dawn's mind, but she had only to think of Clarissa showing her mother a deeply skinned knee to snap her back to the truth of the afternoon.

"Ms. Williams, who's gonna take care of Ebony's stuff?" Jamel asked with just fifteen minutes left in the day. Ebony's backpack, a drawstring bag sneakers came in, was on her chair instead of in her locker and what looked like her wrinkled homework assignment sat on her desk.

"I'll have to," Dawn told him.

When she walked into the main office to drop off Ebony's bag (she had neatly torn up Ebony's homework and deposited it in the trash), Ebony was seated, her long legs stretching toward the closed door of Principal Anderson. Beside her sat a large black woman, her thighs spilling over the sides of the small plastic chair. She could have been Ebony's sister from her face, full cheeks and smooth skin free of makeup, but the lines of worry from her forehead to her chin told Dawn that she was grown. Kids didn't know you could feel a thousand ways about just one thing. Ebony turned as Dawn walked past her, but never said a word.

★ ★ ★

Dawn got out the good plates for dinner on election night in hopes of Schwartz's victory. She had kept pamphlets with her at all times to drop in unexpected places, the chicken wing place in Far Northeast, the farecard machines at Metro Center, and the feminine-products aisle at CVS.

In her voting booth that morning, she clicked the small metal lever next to Carol Schwartz's name. When she pulled the large red handle to cast the vote, it sounded like vindication. Outside of the polling station, the Barry supporters, shrouded in hats and long-sleeved "Barry for Mayor" T-shirts, advanced on her with "Sister" and buttons. Dawn refused both.

Michael surveyed the set table. "I think this is more than we did for our anniversary."

"The race is pretty tight. I'm keeping this on until it

falls off," Dawn told him. She pressed a finger into the I VOTED sticker on her cotton T-shirt.

"Got it. Expect to see that in bed tonight."

Dawn poured them both wine. "Ebony and that new girl got into it today. Seems like Ebony kicked her."

"Oh?" Michael picked up lids from warm pots.

"Yeah. Principal Anderson thought some of her behavior is because of her home circumstances. Single mother. Southeast."

Michael leaned against the counter and folded his arms, a smile slashed across his face. "That's what you think too."

"No. I don't."

"Okay."

"I don't."

"Okay."

"She has real problems that girl, and yes, sometimes we don't want to address them because of where someone comes from. Call out what's really happening. Like people are voting for Barry just because he's black. And Ebony is a mess of a little girl. A real mess and she's been making my entire life hell these last couple of months."

"Why don't you just quit?" Michael said. "Why are you staying there?"

"I like kids."

"You keep convincing yourself that means something, just like that principal, people all over the city for that matter, think being from Southeast means something."

"Easy to say when you're from exactly nowhere."

"I just don't stigmatize where I'm from."

"Why would someone who grew up privileged have to worry about stigma? About somebody deciding what you were capable of because of what blocks you walked to get back to your family?"

"You're right. Okay? You're right." Michael walked out of the kitchen into the living room. Growing up, they fought in her house. Not abuse, not "call Child and Family Services" fought, but nobody was bothered by getting into it. Her parents, from what Dawn could remember. She and Tanya. Tanya and Ma. She and Ma. She and Tanya and Ma. Michael didn't fight. She admired the restraint, until she didn't.

Michael turned on the television.

Jim Vance was anchoring the election coverage. Dawn's mother used to joke that maybe she should've married Jim Vance, but her father had been many of the things Jim Vance was, charming and flawed. They had all been excited to be Washingtonians in the Barry era: her parents, Jim Vance. When Dawn's mother had the news on, Jim Vance explained the world to her in a baritone absent from the alto and soprano chorus of her home. They had always eaten dinner in front of the television, local and national news before the sitcoms came on. After dinner, her mother smoked and drank cola, and Dawn and Tanya drank cola and ate ice cream. Dawn had forsaken sugar in her twenties and grown appalled by her mother's nutritional parenting. But tonight, at the Giant, she had bought a pint of strawberry.

Dawn brought Michael his plate instead of scolding that they needed to eat at the dining table.

"Thank you," Michael said.

"I read some more about the home-buyer program. Some things we'll need to start on soon."

"Have we decided to do that?" He forked through the contents of his plate.

Election coverage was beginning and Dawn could have missed Michael's question watching the reporter at the polling station she'd gone to in Shepherd Park. "Have we . . ."

"Decided. Didn't think we were sure."

"We want to buy a house. We talked about this. I told my mother after we'd talked about this."

"Well, that's part of it. I'm thinking, maybe your mother's right."

"About what?"

"Like rethinking the plan, that there are other things for us to consider first."

Dawn had never imagined a moment of proposal. Since she did not jump rope, she knew none of the rhymes that promised the unfolding of your whole life just because you chanted in a chorus with other girls. "First comes love, then comes marriage" was the only one she could think of, and that wasn't even double Dutch. But the girls had chanted one the other day, something about spelling out the name of the one you loved and Dawn did, quick in her head, twice.

"Probably we should just keep renting, see what happens, before we tie ourselves down to a house." Michael nodded as he took an overlarge bite of food.

Dawn hadn't met Michael's family. The one time

he'd told her his mother was in town, he assured her she wouldn't want to come. "So stuck-up," he'd said. Dawn wondered what his mother knew of her, her upbringing, her education, her job. When they made love, Michael sometimes whispered in her ear to talk like she was *really* from DC. She moaned her authenticity for him, then covered herself after.

"If it's not what you want—"

"I think we just adjust the plan a little."

"As long as we have a plan."

Michael nodded and chewed through a new bite. "Definitely. Schwartz is making a really good showing."

"Yeah." Dawn watched the percentages at the bottom of the screen increase. "They just want the best."

Michael fell asleep after dinner, his neck arched back to rest his head on the couch. The returns were still being counted, but they had a projection.

Jim Vance told her that their new mayor was Marion Barry. He was called a phoenix rising from the ashes. It was said to be the most unlikely turnaround in political history. They said no one could have predicted such a feat just a few short years ago. Dawn didn't know what she would do with all the "Schwartz for Mayor" pamphlets she had.

The phone rang. Dawn got up from the couch and answered already knowing who was calling.

"I know this isn't what you wanted," Ma said. Dawn opened the freezer to get out the strawberry ice cream.

"This wasn't how the night was supposed to go. I don't understand how that's the kind of person who gets everything they want." Barry got to the mic and wiped his brow. "We did it," he told his screaming supporters. "Some people didn't believe in us," he said, "but we believed." Barry's new wife, Cora, was right by his side.

"You watching?"

"Yeah." Dawn sat down on the floor with the pint and a spoon.

"You know she and Effi were friends, right?" Ma said. "Before. During his trial. She sat next to her."

"She did?"

"Yeah, you don't remember?" Ma asked.

"They don't seem like the same kind of people," Dawn said. She moved closer to the television.

"You never know who are the same kind of people."

Dawn didn't respond because when the news cut away to show supporters around the city, in Southeast, Dawn swore one of the little brown girls dancing and chanting "We won, we won" on camera was Ebony.

***

"We can't say exactly who did what. Although we have our suspicions," Principal Anderson told the morning staff meeting. A jumble of voices started, a dozen individual conversations about one thing. Principal Anderson wasn't concerned with election results. Most schoolyard scuffles didn't require anyone else to know but the principal and the parent, but blood was drawn and the school was zero tolerance.

"What does Ebony say happened?" Mrs. Brown asked.

"That she didn't do anything," Principal Anderson said. "She won't tell me what happened, but she keeps asking if I believe her."

"Girls are worse than boys," Mr. Espinoza added. "I keep telling you." The room shook with laughter, a female hand swatted in the direction of Mr. Espinoza.

"Best case, she's suspended. Worst case, special permission is revoked." Principal Anderson tapped a pencil with an oversized #1 eraser on the conference table.

"Ebony's not perfect," Mrs. Brown said to the group, campaigning from her usual seat opposite Principal Anderson. "Both girls could have . . ." Mrs. Brown rushed her hands together to show motion, and many of the teachers nodded their heads in agreement. Then she leaned in to the other black teachers, Dawn seated just beside them all, to garner support. "We don't want to see the girl get moved out of Watson. She probably just needs some help from her teacher."

"I saw Ebony kick her," Dawn said. The words trickled out. A faucet turned on somewhere inside of her, and then the unexpected blast of accusation was too strong to shut off. Heads turned from the first word, trying to locate the unfamiliar sound of Dawn's voice. Some faces swung around the room still looking for the source of the noise. Dawn almost wanted to do the same. It was like when she first started teaching and kept wishing that someone else would start speaking and take the burden off of her. There was nothing to do at the front of the classroom but to keep talking. So what if you didn't know exactly what you were saying? So what if you didn't really know what lesson you were trying to teach? You had to finish the lecture you started.

"You saw her?" Mrs. Brown turned around in her chair and stared at Dawn. She warned Dawn that day to keep a watch on her girls, and for the first time Dawn didn't know if she saw what happened. If Mrs. Brown was going to shame her later, Dawn had to shame Mrs. Brown now.

"Ebony is a troublemaker," Dawn said. "You all know it." She returned Mrs. Brown's stare when she said this. Then she stood up in front of her chair. She would make no concessions.

"You didn't tell me this." Principal Anderson reclined in her seat and waited.

"I hoped Ebony would own up to her mistake," Dawn said. "We all have to take responsibility for our actions." She searched the room of constituents for those who would back her. She got a few nods of understanding and validation.

"Well, if we know what happened—" Principal Anderson began.

"I know," Dawn said. She nodded to Principal Anderson and said "I know" over and over to different faces in the room, campaigning for their trust.

"We revoke special permission," Principal Anderson said. She unhooked the middle button of her jacket. The fabric slackened, as did her face.

Mrs. Brown mumbled to the other teachers, but the noise in Dawn's head overwhelmed her. She could not quiet it anymore than she could her kids. Dawn sat and they continued with recess assignments.

At the end of the meeting, Dawn got up to leave, but Principal Anderson motioned at her with the pencil. The room cleared. Principal Anderson took off her dark-framed glasses and rested them on top of a stack of papers.

"You, I'm sure, have been a wonderful example to Ebony, but in education, and I'm sure you're learning, Dawn, not everyone can be saved. We have to reserve our efforts for those who will, well, pay off in the end. Invest in the ones who will show a profit." She put her glasses back on, as if the declaration had required temporary blindness.

Dawn's mother always told her that grade school in Southeast was safer, even though everyone said the crime rate was higher, but maybe her mother knew that other neighborhoods, even tree-lined ones like Shepherd Park, were unsafe too.

Dawn walked toward the door. Out a faculty-lounge window, wind whipped the leaves on the sidewalk. Parents dropped their children off for the start of the school day. Clarissa stepped onto the sidewalk and waved to someone just past the view of the window. Clarissa began to walk, then stopped and turned. Ebony ran up and put her arm through Clarissa's. Dawn waited for Clarissa to snatch her arm away or for Ebony to push her down. Instead, fat drops of rain fell and the girls ran together toward the front door, out of Dawn's view.

The rain meant no girls would be outside at recess

lining up for double Dutch. When she was a girl, Dawn thought she didn't like jumping, but jumping wasn't so different from leaping from square to square in hop-scotch. It wasn't the jumping, it was what you jumped to, all those promises of a new day. Little girls thought all they had to do was want something enough and they could have it. Ask for it at the top of their lungs in chorus and it would be theirs, but you couldn't stay inside the ropes, hoping and wishing. Dawn knew now why the game was so hard, the ropes swinging in and out, back and forth. Getting in was treacherous—starting something—but getting out was worse. The ropes would savage you. It was hard to see the escape route and how to land unscathed on the other side of the cage.

ALL THE THINGS YOU'LL NEVER DO

Bess liked to wear her uniform to Chuck and Billie's Restaurant and Bar for Long Island Iced Tea Thursdays. She could have changed in those all-automated bathrooms in the airport terminal if she felt like it, so that she wouldn't have to use the nasty one in the TSA breakroom. She could have just walked in with some tight jeans on and ordered a drink, as if she was just anybody, as if she worked just anywhere.

The lights at C and B's were turned down so low, people probably could only half see her uniform until somebody opened up the door and let in the early evening light. Nothing like her building at National Airport, with windows that stretched from sidewalk to sun and stone floors shined and buffed to reflect your footsteps.

The woman sitting next to Bess at the bar looked at her badge. "Since 9/11," Bess told her and leaned in with a smile, "there was almost no more important job."

"All these attacks now, too? People you wouldn't

believe going out of this city are going through me. And people at the airport can be straight-up nasty. Here they come, complaining about how slow the security line is, wondering why they can't take their water in with them, asking if they really gotta take off their shoes. And with those full-body scanners? I don't hear the end of that shit. Go take a bus, I tell them. You know?" New York and Richmond could be reached within four hours. That was far enough.

She signaled to the bartender to set her up another one.

"The other day, I get this bama who can't find his damn ID. His leg is broken, right, so he's already taking all his damn time to get to the front of the line. And then, here he is, searching all over, patting down his jacket and shit. Can't find it though. But, for all that, he's holding up my line. Inconsiderate, you know? Other people are trying to go places too, see the world and all. He don't care though."

Bess took a long sip and set her hand on the scuffed bar. She liked to get her nails done, but she kept them short because no woman who's going somewhere has nails so long she could scratch somebody just from shaking their damn hand.

"So then I tell him he needs to stand aside, you know, that he's getting in other people's way. But he won't leave. Instead, he starts saying, 'No, no, I've got it, I know I've got it.' Real snooty-like. 'Just wait,' he keeps telling me. So, I do, because I'm there to serve people, you know, and he don't understand that. He thinks I'm there because, you know, it's like a good time for me on Thursday morning or whatever. But once I decide to go ahead and give him that time, he finally pulls his ID out of you'll never guess where."

The woman was still listening, Bess was pretty sure, but she was looking at Bess in the mirror behind the bar. She wasn't even looking in her face, but this was how people were raised these days, how people thought they could treat you any kind of way. Bess sipped on her drink. She should stop even talking to her, not tell her the punch line. But no, she should hear this story, she should understand just how much life demanded of Bess. This girl probably didn't know a thing about demands.

"He reaches into his cast, right? His cast. And pulls out this sweaty, bent-up piece of mess. Hands it to me like it ain't nothing. Proud of himself even. But I got him though, because I wrote on his boarding pass. I got them to search him. I got authority to do that, to make sure people are gonna be safe from sketchiness like that."

She must not have heard Bess, because she didn't look as impressed as she should have. Her head did finally start to nod, but real slow, like she couldn't even understand all the things Bess was talking about, all the things she knew. But then something in her look did change, and Bess sat up straighter in the chair, as straight as she could with those Long Islands starting to weigh her down, and got ready for some respect.

"You go to high school with me?" The woman pushed her bangs to the side and turned toward Bess. She brought her face in close. "Right? Class of '15?"

And then Bess saw it too: recognition limping into the bar and sitting too damn close, making her uncomfortable.

"Maybe. High school is a long way from the stuff I'm doing now."

"You was with Rich, right? Didn't y'all have a baby?"

Bess got pregnant their senior year. She didn't hear the end of her mother's mouth about it. "Why you go and do that?" she'd asked her over and over.

"Why you working at the airport?" she asked. Now, she wouldn't stop looking at Bess.

"Where do you work?" Bess asked. She wished for a pen and a boarding pass.

"Human resources for DC government," she said. Her bangs fell back in her eyes.

"DC government." Bess let out a laugh.

A lot of the people she graduated high school with were working those same dumb-ass jobs. Just like Rich. Talking about he was going to support them, saying they would get a house. All he was ever going to do was work a DC government job, move up a pay scale, never leave his job, and never have to. No one got fired. Bess didn't do the exact same shit every day like they did, filling out the same forms, pressing the same damn computer keys in those old-ass buildings. Not her. This girl was hiring other dumb-ass people to work those dumb-ass jobs. Couldn't waste your life much more than that.

"You get to fly free or something like that?" the girl said. "That'd make working that job worth it. I'd go as many places as I can."

"I don't work for the airlines. I work for the federal government. Department of Homeland Security. I don't just work for some airline."

"Oh, okay. Well, I guess that's good."

"I know it is. I know what I'm doing," Bess said. She waved for her third Long Island and mean mugged the girl in the mirror behind the bar.

Someone turned the music up and R&B blared out of scratchy-sounding speakers. Bess sang along. She didn't really know the words, she didn't even know the name of the song.

She forgot all about her day and all about that girl from high school. Bess didn't even notice when she left because by then she was slow dragging with the tallest, finest motherfucker in there. She dug the pads of her fingers into the waves he'd probably worn a durag for every chance he got to get them right for the weekend. His back hunched over hers. His slippery smooth words landed on her earlobe. She closed her eyes to catch the tone, not the meaning, and watched the dollar bills suspended from the ceiling sway with the damp heat until the song ended.

***

Unlike that girl from high school, Bess didn't work Monday through Friday. But this Friday morning, she wished it was the last day of her week. Her hair was still smoky from cigarettes and her eyes were bleary from all those drinks. Somewhere in the pants pocket of her uniform was her cell phone with the number of the dude she danced with all night. She couldn't remember his name. She wanted to sleep in and wait for the baby to wake up in another hour. Bess wobbled over to his crib. Her mother said the baby could just sleep in the bed with her, but Bess had wanted to get him something of his own. She hated when people didn't do right by their kids.

Will was in the Batman pajamas that Bess found in Salvation Army, new with tags still on. He always kicked his blanket off, his dark toes searching for a breeze. It was what his father did, airing just his toes to cool him down. Bess didn't cover up Rich, he was a man, but she did cover up Will. He, at least, was still her baby. She leaned down and pressed her lips into the pillow of his cheek. The mobile of airplanes suspended from the ceiling turned above him and she gave it an extra push.

One day, she'd have more space: their own apartment, a whole playroom for Will with Batman everything, and a big bedroom so she could keep an ironing board up all the time.

Even on days when she didn't work, Bess ironed her uniform. She knew to turn the pants inside out because black polyester would get shiny and make you look stupid if you didn't. She made creases in the legs, spraying the starch on thick and coating not just the pants but the ironing board and her nearby hand. Her mother would buy whatever starch was on sale. Bess didn't go for that. She bought the expensive starch, one that came in a can with waterfalls and rivers on it. She didn't know what waterfalls had to do with getting her pants crisp, but that stuff did it every time. Starch went on the shirt too, but she made sure not to put any creases in the sleeves. It made you look corny. Some of the other TSA agents came in looking like that, shirt all crazy with creases and pants halfway wrinkled. They probably didn't even use the cheap starch. They probably didn't use starch at all.

You couldn't be in charge in wrinkled clothes.

"You gonna be late," her mother said. She leaned on the frame of the doorway. Her hair wrapped and pinned from sleep. She wore the same housedress she had since Bess was a child.

Bess put her finger to her lips and thumbed at the crib.

"I'll be fine," she said. She went back to ironing the sleeves of her shirt.

"What time you got in?"

"Don't know, but I needed to relax. When you got authority in a job, you also got stress."

"Hm." Her mother pursed her lips like she was about to spit something out. "Been meaning to tell you Rich called, said he could take the baby more, give you time to get used to your new job."

"He's not taking Will."

"Let him be a father." Time was when her mother hated Rich, said Bess had gotten knocked up by a fool. Now, she acted like Bess was in the wrong.

"He messed that up." Bess pulled on her pants and zipped them. She put her arms through the still-warm shirtsleeves.

"He got the steadier income. Will could have a room all his own over there."

"I know what I'm doing." Bess buttoned her shirt and kissed Will again before she left.

★ ★ ★

Bess and Vincent got stuck with loading bags in the back for the morning shift. Some people liked being with the checked luggage or behind the scanner, just watching the x-rayed bags roll past. They didn't want to talk to anyone. Bess wanted to be in the front, checking the boarding passes and IDs. Passengers respected that first person they met more. Some people would look nervous like they were waiting for her to say that they couldn't go through, or they'd look real close at what she wrote on their boarding pass, worried that she thought they'd done something wrong.

Vincent stopped after picking up the biggest bag so far that morning. He pressed one hand into his over-sized middle-aged belly. He'd been a handler for fifteen years, loading bags, but when the TSA started looking for people willing to take the five-hundred-question government test, he applied. The background checks and running his credit report, they didn't matter. "An exquisite opportunity," he told Bess.

She liked that. She hated people who didn't ever try new shit. Rich never wanted to try anything. Chicken and steak were all he ever ate. He told her he'd had salmon once before, but he'd pronounced it *SAL-mon* and Bess hadn't needed much more than that to know she was done. When she left Rich's place that day, she went to her mother's house in Northeast. While Will played with his Tonka truck on the kitchen linoleum, Bess took out the TSA information sheet she'd printed at the library and pressed it flat on the table. "I got plans," she told her mother. "I know it," her mother said. "But is this plan like the others or is this one going to work?"

Bess wheeled two uprights closer to the large scanning machine and tossed them one by one onto it. Dirty-ass bags. She wiped her hands together, careful to not wipe them on her uniform.

"People just want to complain, talk shit. Like I was telling this know-nothing last night, this lady kept asking me all these questions about the job. You ever get that?" she asked.

"Sure, sometimes. Curiosity is the lust of the mind," he said.

"Uh-huh. Anyway, I tell this lady last night, bugging me with the questions, if these people trying to fly don't like it, go take a bus. They don't check you," Bess said.

"Buses won't get you across water," Vincent said. "And there's still something about the takeoff of a jet engine, being thirty thousand feet in the air."

"Yeah?" Bess asked.

"You don't like flying?"

"Don't know. Never been on a plane," Bess said. Vincent got quiet, and Bess felt like she could hear the words like he heard them, and she didn't think she much liked the sound.

"You want to though? Right?" Vincent stopped loading bags again. "You'll go to Florida for the new training?"

"Yeah, they paying, I go. And, I mean, I think about flying, you know. I'm not like these people who don't never want to go anywhere. Went to high school with this girl who hadn't even been on the Metro. Stayed in her same dumb neighborhood," Bess said. "That's not me." When she'd left Rich and told him his life wasn't going anywhere, he'd asked where hers was going. And he kept asking while she carried Will and a duffel bag stuffed with their things down five flights of stairs.

"Be careful with those bags," Vincent said. "Make sure they're—"

"I know what I'm doing," Bess said.

***

Fridays were the goddamn worst, the business travelers trying to get home for the weekend and the families and couples trying to get away. The afternoons were all the international people, coming for their overnight flights to London and Rome. These women always did it up more than the domestic fliers, more scarves and prettier shoes. Sometimes they wheeled bags Bess had never seen before, not just some plain black roller bags. They had bags in different colors with brand names on them. Or they carried weathered leather bags, big and deep when they reached in for their passports. She knew these women had jobs where someone called them Ms., where someone waited for their approval. Bess marked their papers just like she would mark any of the others. One Ms. stepped up to the stand and gave Bess not one but two pieces of paper. She clicked the pen.

"ID," Bess said.

"You have it," she said. Bess thought the accent might be British, or maybe she was supposed to say English. Vincent had given her some history lesson on the difference last week, but he was on break. Bess looked at the papers the woman had. One was the boarding pass and the other was a letter with a crest stamped at the top.

"Ma'am, I need a photo ID. This doesn't qualify." Bess held the paper out to Ms.

"My passport was stolen, so I've had my embassy declare that I am a citizen and should be allowed on board," she said. She pulled at the knot in her scarf.

"I don't think that's enough to get you on the plane," Bess said.

"Well, I was told it was."

Vincent wouldn't be back from break for another five minutes.

"You can't just . . . it's not enough."

"Do you know that?" she asked. Her nails were short and painted a pale pink. She tapped her fingers on the top of Bess's stand. Around her wrist was one slim silver bracelet. On her finger was a wedding ring with diamonds all around.

"I know what I'm doing," Bess said. She gave the woman back her pieces of paper.

"The embassy assured me."

"I won't let you through," Bess said. "You'll need to move away from the security desk." She smiled at the next person in line, hoping they would step forward.

"You don't know what you're talking about."

"Ma'am, you need to step aside." Bess motioned for the man at the front of the line, but he still didn't step up.

Ms. didn't reply, only draped her other hand over the stand.

"Ma'am, you're going to have to step aside," Bess said. "Sir, come forward." The man finally neared the stand.

"You're very disrespectful."

Ms. moved in front of the man and directly in front of Bess, but Bess leaned away so she could still focus on the man.

"You should be fired for treating someone this way," Ms. said, her voice just like Bess's high school teachers when they were trying to embarrass her, trying to let her know that nobody but them was in charge.

"Ma'am." She tried to reach around to take the documents from the man, to move things along.

"Where is the head TSA person?" the woman asked.

"The head TSA person?" Bess asked. She hated people who couldn't get their sentences together.

"Your supervisor, dear. You don't know what you're doing," Ms. said.

The man who had been waiting behind Ms. lowered

his ID, like he wasn't going to give it to Bess anymore, like she didn't know how to check him. The people behind him started moving into the other screener lines. One woman shook her head at Bess like she should be ashamed or something. Another looked away when she looked him in the eye, just like that girl from high school being disrespectful, acting like she knew anything about her. She heard someone in line say something about getting a supervisor, just like Ms. wanted.

Ms.'s dark bob swayed with her movements to find someone behind Bess. She removed her hands from the stand and began walking toward one of the scanning lines. On her way, she bumped into Bess's arm, the sleeve stitched with the Transportation Security Administration patch.

"I haven't cleared you. You can't go through there," Bess said. But the woman didn't stop, so Bess grabbed at her shoulder.

"Do not do that," she said, looking over her shoulder only at Bess's left hand.

Bess didn't move her hand and the woman tried to keep walking. Her shirt was silk. Bess could tell because she'd gone into one of the shops at National Airport, one where the male business travelers stopped to get their wives something, and fingered a dress in there and the label said "100% silk." Bess didn't know if you ironed that with starch. Maybe Ms. always got it dry-cleaned. Maybe she had someone at her house who did those things for her, someone who made her life better and easier because Ms. had already worked so hard and smiled and shaken so many important people's hands that at the end of the day she couldn't think about something as small as clothes. Bess hated people who couldn't do anything for themselves but thought they could do everything. Bess hated people who didn't know what they were doing.

She grabbed the woman's other shoulder and began to pull her back. The woman twisted her body and pulled at Bess's hands, but she would not let go.

"I haven't cleared you," Bess said over and over.

Ms. didn't have the authority that Bess did. She couldn't just do whatever she wanted. Bess heard the soft rip of the silk and the woman's shrill "Get off!" right before the commands of two other TSA agents for her to do the same.

★★★

Waiting to see someone took hours, but the final meeting with a supervisor so high up Bess hadn't even seen him yet took only minutes. The woman was important, not just a citizen of the country with the crest emblazoned on their stationary, but a special assistant to the ambassador. It had been the ambassador's call that ended it for Bess. The TSA didn't want more bad publicity. The supervisor used words like *charges* and *outraged* and *disgrace*. She hadn't known the rules at all. He wasn't sure she'd listened in her training. She should have accepted the paper, and if she wasn't sure then she should have called a supervisor. When the woman tried to walk through security, Bess should have motioned to the next closest TSA officer to intercept her. Most certainly, she shouldn't have restrained her as she did. She shouldn't have torn at her clothes, called her names. Bess hadn't called her anything, even if she had wanted to. She hated people who lied.

The guards instructed to escort her out asked for the uniform.

"But it's all I have," Bess told the men. Still, she loosened the tie and unbuttoned her shirt, the badge weighed down the starched cotton. They stared at her in her black tank top.

Before she walked out, she looked for Vincent. Any evidence of her scuffle with Ms. was gone. The passengers lined up in irritation once again. Vincent checked and scribbled and smiled. She wanted to tell him goodbye, but she didn't want to yell. She didn't want to hear her voice amplified over the marble and three-story-high windows. She hated people who didn't know their place.

It was still early as she drove home, and if she went directly there, her mother would ask if something had happened. If she went and drank some Long Islands without her uniform on, no one at Chuck and Billie's would know who she was. So, she got out of the 395 tunnel at the first exit and waited at a red light.

MAMBO SAUCE

He had good bones, the archways of his arms when he hugged her, the strong lines of his frame. Constance met him at a bar in Brooklyn. Brian wasn't who she had been looking for, in a place she didn't frequent. A black woman in a mostly white bar talking to a white guy over white music she didn't know. She marveled at his views nonetheless, the intellectual skyline dotted with feminism, prison reform, and progressive economic policy. The negotiations that night took so long she began to wonder if she were making a mistake. He wanted to go out Friday night. She thought Friday was too large a commitment to make. She argued for Sunday brunch. He countered with Saturday night. She held firm: Sunday brunch. Final offer. They shook on it, and when she tried to pull away he held on to her hand and she remembered the good bones, the sturdiness missing from the lean-to men she had dated before.

He became hers. She owned him outright, paid in full. He said so in the midst of a weekend sleepover.

"I should post a sign," he told her, his finger tracing

the lines of a rectangle on the left side of his chest. "Property of Constance."

"Is this what you expected?" she said.

"You're what I've been looking for."

"Exactly?" she asked. She had seen pictures of his ex-girlfriends. He had dated black women before, he told her that first night. Dated black women before, sure, but he had never had a black girlfriend—that word so precious it had been like a child asking for a toy when he first used it to introduce her to a friend.

"Yes. Exactly."

Ownership had been her lifelong dream, not that he didn't require some improvements, the rickety way he told jokes and the creak of a man who at thirty-five strummed a guitar and told stories about the band he had always wanted to start. He got a new job in DC as a charter-school lobbyist and asked if she would come with him. It had only been six months, but Constance surveyed their landscape, even the rockiness of their interracial terrain, took in the height of their possibilities, and said yes. She could always unload him if she decided to move on, but for now, she was invested.

And in DC, Constance could be different. She wouldn't be the part-time teacher and full-time dreamer she had been in New York. She could pursue art, call herself an artist. Brian insisted on it, that she take the time she needed to sculpt and find her voice. Once, Brian had gotten out of bed in the middle of the night, naked and hair tousled, to touch each of the pieces Constance had sculpted. "And what's this one?" he said. "And this?" he asked. He came back to bed and she told him, his face close enough that she could whisper and even then, she felt that if she hadn't spoken the words he would have heard them anyway. She told him about her first sculptures and what impossible work it was until what was once only in her mind formed itself in the world. "You form it," he'd said. He listened and then asked questions, his eyes closing when he did, searching for the right phrase. And one time with his eyes closed, she had mouthed *love* when it was much too early to think such a word, much less press lips, even soundless ones, into forming it. Now, they said that word to each other all the time. Him, first. Him, most often.

★★★

The broker took them all over DC, but the neighborhoods where they really wanted to live—Adams Morgan, Dupont Circle, Shaw—were all out of their price range. Brian had gone to Georgetown but told Constance from the beginning that wasn't the neighborhood for them. They finally found an apartment in Far Northeast, the broker assuring them that the neighborhood was up-and-coming.

"I haven't seen many white people," Constance told Brian after their first visit to the place.

Brian said only, "This place gets so much light." He fingered the old window casements in the apartment and smiled.

The second time she brought it up, over Ethiopian food in Shaw, she asked, "And you'll be comfortable there?"

"My king bed won't fit, but that thing's old anyway and your queen is enough space for us." Brian tore off more injera; he scooped up some of the doro wat with the spongy bread. He swallowed the mouthful and after he sucked on each food-stained finger, he smiled.

The third time, she finally said it outright because she had to be sure. "We're the only interracial couple in the neighborhood," she said.

He laughed. "Connie, how many couples have you seen? The neighborhood is changing. I'm sure we won't be the only ones." Constance was unconvinced. Brian moved toward her, stroking her close-cropped hair. "And so what if we were?"

They moved in the next week. Her parents sent a gift card to help them decorate their new home and promises of coming to visit from California. Her mother had been surprised by Constance's worry about dating a white guy. Her mother was more surprised to discover she hadn't dated one before.

"I always kind of thought that was you," she had told Constance. She yelled to Constance's father just then, a *what* that was impatient and harsh. "I'll have to call you later," her mother said before hanging up and before Constance could ask what her mother had seen in her. She liked living in New York because she could find mixed crowds and parties where she didn't have to skillfully work her body to the ground like other black women could. As a girl in San Francisco, she hadn't learned to do that. Rock and pop had been the soundtrack to her teenage years, when she was just as likely to sing into the hairbrush of her Chinese American best friend as the hair pick of her black one.

Brian's mother—his father dead since he was a teenager—sent love and a hundred-dollar bill in a card from Virginia. She wrote inside, *You'll get the real money when I can call Connie my daughter-in-law*. Brian laughed.

"How long should I tell her that will take?" he asked Constance. She was hanging their curtains.

"Is that at the right height?" she asked, but before he could answer, the rod fell to the floor, heavy with its own weight.

★★★

The first day of Brian's job, Constance began sculpting not long after he left, eager to have something to show him when he got home. Four hours in and she had progressed little. She wandered a circuitous path through their apartment. Brian had a beat-up car that he'd kept in New York, mostly for major grocery store runs, that she could use. She didn't want to drive. In Brooklyn, she walked all the time. One block became ten and she could peer into the open windows of brownstones or eavesdrop on the closest sidewalk conversation.

She got out of their apartment and onto their block, the silence of this city foreign to her. She turned onto a major street and was the only one walking. People waited at a bus stop, the Metro wasn't close. Brian biked the distance and he must have gotten stares on his route. The blocks of the neighborhood had few businesses: a check-cashing place, a Chinese carry-out, a furniture-rental store. Then, across the street, Constance saw a pink-and-white striped awning with script that read *Winging It!*

Inside the chicken joint, the air felt heavy with grease. The paint saturated with it. The floor waxed with it. This was where the neighborhood was at lunchtime on a Monday: crowding together to put in orders for fried chicken and fries. The cost of two wings and fries was laughable, only two dollars and twenty-five cents. The price was once lower, the *$2.25* written on paper that had been taped over the last price. One of the women behind the counter was at least in her forties or fifties, another might have been as young as twenty, and a third woman looked to be in her sixties. Age was always hard to tell with black folk.

People clumped together with no sense of a line, but the women, especially the oldest one, knew who was next, as if an invisible number popped up above their head when the bell above the door announced their arrival. The women would point and ask, "What you want, honey?" A short and stout light-skinned man tended most of the fryers, setting them down into the bubbling grease. The women lifted them up and drained them. They tonged the freshly fried chicken into checkerboard-patterned baskets and then held one large salt and one large pepper shaker above the food. Some of the customers, mostly men, simply nodded for the seasonings. Others said "Everything," and then the women would reach for a bottle of hot sauce too. Constance stood back, she didn't want to come off as a newcomer. She had hit the tail end of the rush it seemed, and once most of the customers cleared, it was her, one burly man up to his elbows in his meal, an older gentleman sitting on one of the few stools in the small place, and the staff.

"Honey?" one of the women asked. She pointed the same finger at Constance she had at everyone else.

"Three chicken wings and fries." The woman nodded and the fry cook dropped a new basket in.

"Best wings in DC," the older gentleman said to her. He moved the brim of his hat up to wipe sweat from his forehead.

"Smells like it," Constance said back.

"Never been here before?" he asked. He had a cane and he leaned into it to get nearer to her. Constance shook her head. She glanced at the women to make sure that wasn't a problem.

"What you doing over here, honey?" the oldest woman asked. Her voice was sly and soft. She wiped the counter down, but kept her eyes on Constance.

"I just moved here," she said. She had thought *we*, but the sentence came out with an *I*.

"From where? Over in Northwest?" one of the other women, the youngest and chubbiest, asked. She had curls under her hairnet.

"No, from out of the city," she said. The burly man eating his chicken turned with a ketchup-laden fry in his hand.

"Baltimore or something?" the young chubby one kept up with her questions.

"New York," Constance said, and then, "Brooklyn, actually." It felt like it would give her more credibility.

"Where Brooklyn at?" the young girl rapped, mimicking the famous hip hop line. She laughed and hit the fry cook in the back. He only grunted.

"That girl got too much energy for her own good," the oldest one said to Constance. Constance smiled at the ease between them.

"Well, it's so nice to see some young, single sisters in the neighborhood," the older gentleman said. He winked at her. The women dissolved into laughter. Their shoulders shook with amusement and their heads shook in disbelief.

"Let me find out Mr. Bruce is in here trying to get himself a young girl," the third woman, who had kept quiet until then, said. She was tall and slight, all angles in her white uniform. Under her hairnet, she had a bun of what looked like fake hair on top of her head. "He got a chance?" the woman asked Constance, trying to get her in on the joke. She was eager to join the sorority.

"He might be too much man for me," Constance said. She had wanted a good line that was also a little bawdy, and the women loved it. They responded in choruses of elongated "Girl" and then "You ain't never lied."

Mr. Bruce did his part by sitting up taller on his stool and tapping his cane on the scuffed linoleum. The oldest one slowed her laughing enough to raise the fry basket and put Constance's food in a container.

"Everything," Constance said. The woman smiled and nodded her approval, she sprinkled hot sauce on generously.

"You want mambo too?" she asked. Constance didn't know what that was and couldn't be sure if she'd said *mambo* or *mumbo*.

"She from New York, she don't know about mambo sauce," the young one said. She grabbed a couple of small plastic containers full of red sauce from a nearby counter. "Try it." She opened one and offered it to Constance, who dipped a finger in and put it in her mouth. It was sweet and spicy, like duck sauce and hot sauce combined. She wasn't sure she liked it, but the woman offered it again. Constance took another finger full, and liked it better that time. She nodded and grabbed two more containers and put them into a paper bag with her food. Constance reached into her pocket for some cash. She would bet they didn't take cards.

"Go on," the oldest one said. "Welcome to the neighborhood." She pushed the bag toward her.

"No, it's so cheap already. I can't let you do that."

"She said go on," the tall one said.

"Maybe we'll get Mr. Bruce to pay for it. He can't let his new girlfriend starve," the youngest said. They rocked with laughter again. Constance joined in and took her food.

"See you tomorrow," someone said just as she pushed her way through the door.

She thought of ideas to sculpt almost as soon as

she got back to the house. She reached for her chisel with chicken grease still on her fingers. After half of the second wing and the huge helping of fries, she couldn't eat anymore. Brian gnawed on the last piece of chicken when he came home that night and told her about his day.

"A lot to be done," he said, biting into some fried skin on the wing tip. "But everyone seems up for it."

Constance told him about walking around the neighborhood, but didn't relay her conversation in Winging It! She said only that the people were nice and that when the wings were hot and just out of the fryer, they were even better.

"What's this?" Brian asked, holding up one of the mambo-sauce containers.

"It's this special DC sauce," Constance said. "Try it."

Brian did, but he made a face after. "I don't get it. It's weird."

"I liked it," she said.

"Well you," he said, putting the small containers back into the fridge, "can have all of it."

***

Their first weekend in DC, Brian's old college friends had a welcome dinner for them. Constance found a colorful dress and wore large gold hoop earrings with it. Brian said she looked beautiful, but when they got to the friend's townhouse in Georgetown, Constance felt like she'd come to the wrong party. Everyone else was very casual, cargo shorts or jeans and flip-flops. One of the four women had a dress on, but she was unadorned. The pale pink of the dress was pretty but barely registered between her complexion and light blond hair. They all lived in DC, had ever since they graduated from Georgetown together. A couple were lawyers who went from undergrad to Georgetown Law. There was a teacher, Alissa, who grabbed Constance's hands when Brian said she taught in New York. Someone else worked in government like Brian, and others had corporate jobs that Constance lost track of during the introductions.

They all knew a lot about politics and world events, and made witty and obscure pop culture references some of her Brooklyn girlfriends wouldn't have caught. But the room didn't roll with laughter and Constance noticed early on that there was no music. She was used to get-togethers that ended in old-school Michael Jackson and hip hop that started with, "Six minutes, six minutes, six minutes, Doug E. Fresh, you're on." The home began to empty out, many of the friends saying their good-nights, until it was just Constance and Brian, and Alissa and her husband, Mark.

"You teach, is that right, Connie?" Mark asked. She would have preferred he call her Constance.

"No, she's a sculptor," Brian said. He turned to Constance and she nodded in approval. "Sculptress?"

"I'm a sculptor," she said, smiling at Alissa instead of Mark.

"Does that get lonely? Just you in the apartment, right?" Alissa asked.

"Oh, she gets out sometimes," Brian said. "Connie

brought home this chicken, like the best chicken I've ever had. But then she tries to get me to try this stuff called, wait what is it?" Brian said. He had his hand around a bottle of beer, the other on Constance's knee.

"Mambo sauce," she said, wishing he hadn't brought it up.

"Oh yeah, we call it ghetto sauce," Alissa said. She laughed and the men joined. Constance strained a smile.

"They all talk about it like it's foie gras or something. You don't remember it from college, Bri?" Mark asked. Brian shook his head.

"And where are you guys again?" Alissa asked. "U Street and that area?"

"No. Far Northeast," Brian said.

"God, no idea where that is at all," Alissa said. She turned to Mark for his recognition, but he had none to offer her. "We're so Northwest-bound."

"Well, your part of Capitol Hill is Northeast. And H Street is," Mark offered, parsing the sections of the city.

"And I hear Southwest has really been transforming," Alissa said. Mark nodded.

"We like it over there," Brian said. He squeezed Constance's hand and she limply squeezed his back.

"And it's safe?" Alissa asked. Constance wondered if she had ever even been to the other side of the city.

"Of course," Constance said.

"Any other restaurants besides the fried-chicken place?" Mark asked.

"Lots," Brian said. "The two Chinese carryouts." His friends collapsed in laughter. It was a joke Constance had made to Brian after their first week in the apartment, the place filled with too many boxes to think about cooking and their options limited to chicken wings or shrimp fried rice. The comparisons to their former hip Brooklyn neighborhoods had run roughshod over Far Northeast.

"And I'm sure the liquor store has a fine collection of 40s to choose from," Alissa said.

"Not every neighborhood needs to be Georgetown," Constance said. "Places like this are so," she searched for the right intellectually damning word, "stagnant. I wouldn't choose a place to live just so I could get an ego boost when I told people." Alissa reddened, her face now a better contrast to her pale pink dress.

"I thought that was the only reason people ever moved to New York," Mark said. He took a sip of his beer, but watched Constance over the bottle's rim.

"Well, that's not why I moved there," Constance said. Brian's fingers tapped out a fevered rhythm on her knee.

"People do lots of things for the reaction they get, right?" Mark looked at Constance and Brian's interlocked hands.

"Like that trick we played on Sigma Chi?" Brian said, moving his hand off Constance's knee to offer Mark a high five. Mark pointed a finger at Brian and began laughing.

"Oh man, and your face when we almost got caught." They began to talk over each other to tell the story and Alissa stiffly asked Constance if she wanted anything else.

★ ★ ★

Constance endured another half an hour until finally Brian seemed ready to leave. They said their goodbyes, but Constance held her face away from Mark when he tried to give her a kiss on the cheek. Alissa told Constance she hoped they would see her again soon, but when she said it she looked as if something sharp and sour were contained in her cheeks.

"They're good people," Brian said, when they were in the car and on their way back home.

"I'm sure they are," Constance said.

"Then what was with the Georgetown takedown?" he asked. He pulled up to a red light and turned to face her.

"What about their takedown? And why did you tell them about mambo sauce?" she asked.

"What? They already knew about mambo sauce," he said. The light turned and Brian accelerated, the car jolting forward.

"No, why did you tell them about any of it? The chicken place, my joke about the Chinese carryouts?" she asked. He was driving too fast.

"Why did I make conversation? When clearly you weren't going to?"

"Is this the way we came?" she asked. She peered out at water, but she hadn't remembered any on the way there.

"They're not New Yorkers, okay? But they're still good people," he said. He made a U-turn right before an oncoming car and the horn of the vehicle blared.

"Why do you keep saying they're good people? Like that makes up for being ignorant. *Ghetto sauce*?" she said, yelling this time.

"She didn't mean anything by it. Everyone says *ghetto*."

"I've never heard you say *ghetto*, Brian."

"Well, I've never heard you be a bitch to my friends," he said. He pulled the car over onto a small side street. "I need to goddamn map us back to Northeast."

"I wasn't a bitch. Don't you call me a bitch. You shared something you shouldn't have," she said. "And your friends said things they shouldn't have. Neither of those make me a bitch."

Brian tapped the screen of his phone, his face set aglow with its light and his anger.

"It doesn't even know the address." He typed on his phone, then struck the screen, then banged it on the steering wheel. "We can't even get to the fucking neighborhood, but you want to defend it rather than, for just one night, being nice to my friends?"

"It isn't just one night," Constance said. She turned to look out the window, the lawn of a house before her, a tricycle abandoned until morning. Silence set in.

"No, it isn't. It's a lot of fucking nights," he said. He breathed out. He touched the side of her face, his fingertips on her cheek. "Of us."

Constance hadn't been talking about them. She had been talking about the anger at his friends' ignorance, the lopsidedness of feeling defensive and never knowing when someone was coming to knock her sideways. She had said something about their dismissal of Far Northeast, but had smiled at ghetto sauce. She hadn't bothered to defend loving Brian, to question the look Mark had given. It wasn't just one night of excising the parts of her that didn't create the right picture, a paper doll with cutouts in the right places so that when she was strung up, over archways and doorframes, everyone would be ever so complimentary. It wasn't just one night. Brian was right. It was a lot of fucking nights.

★★★

Constance's second visit to Winging It! was a whole week after the first. She came a little later that day to avoid the rush, and when she walked inside the oldest waitress pointed a finger at her and asked, "Where you been?"

Constance put her hands together as if pleading for forgiveness. "I know. Shame on me."

"See what happen when you give people free food?" It was the first time she heard the fry cook's voice.

"Earl's right," the woman said. Constance, when she had replayed her first visit, named all the ladies in her head after her girlfriends in Brooklyn. The oldest, bossy one was Gina. The young, sweet one was Joy, and the tall and quiet one was Tracy. She hadn't bothered to name the cook, so she subbed in Earl.

"You give someone the best fried chicken they ever laid lips to," Gina said, "and what you get? No visit, no call, no nothing."

Joy shook her head at Constance.

"How about I pay for this meal and the last one to make up for it?" Constance asked.

"Oh, now we need your charity?" Tracy said. They each tried to hold their belligerence, but Gina broke first, laughing off her indignation.

"Come on, what you want?"

Constance walked closer to the counter and relaxed. She ordered fish and asked for everything including the mambo sauce. She'd put some on her eggs one morning, dunked a piece of toast in it the next. They joked with Mr. Bruce again, and Constance found out that the burly, silent customer from last time who was there again was Gina's husband.

"He don't like to talk, and I don't like him to," she said. "It's a match, honey."

Constance laughed with the girls, slapping the counter when someone made an extra-funny joke. Mr. Bruce said he liked Constance eating lots of food. He liked a woman with some thickness. The women joked that he'd have to wait a long time to get that with her.

"Twig, is what she is," Tracy said.

"Look who's talking," Constance shot back. Gina and Joy about died. They slapped each other's backs when they weren't howling into each other's shoulders.

"She think she can come in here talking to anybody any way," Tracy said, but she grinned through the condemnation. "Come on, let's see." Tracy came out from behind the counter and put an arm around Constance. "Call it."

"I don't know, think young Miss might win. She got a little more curve on hers," Joy said.

"What about this though?" Tracy turned around, and the women mm-hmmed.

"Now on that back there," Gina said, motioning for Constance to turn around. "Yup, you got her."

"Give me another order," Constance said. Everyone began to laugh, even Gina's husband.

"What do you do, Twig?" Tracy asked.

"I make art. I'm an artist," Constance said, the words dribbling out of her mouth.

"Like what?" Gina asked.

"You take pictures or something?" Joy asked. She posed with a hand on an errant hip and cast her eyes toward the tile floor. She jumped out of the pose just as quick presenting the palms of her hands to the room in a ta-da.

"No pictures," Constance said, laughing at Joy's enthusiasm.

"I don't know if I can sit long enough for a painting, but I could try." Joy hopped back to her pose and froze.

"I sculpt," Constance finally said.

"Like these statues we got all over this city? You might need to move somewhere else, where there's less competition," Gina said.

"You should do a statue for this place," Mr. Bruce said.

"Shoot, she might as well make you a statue, Mr. Bruce. Don't know the last time you weren't sitting on that stool," Tracy said.

"Ain't that the truth. I open up and seem like he's already sitting there. Sleeping upright in here," Gina said. She and Tracy celebrated their tag-team comedy.

"I could do a statue of Mr. Bruce maybe," Constance said, hoping for Gina and Tracy's approval.

"No cane though, better to capture me when I was in my prime."

"Who says you aren't still?" Constance said. Joy began whooping in approval.

"We could see your work somewhere?" Gina asked.

"Probably in New York, one of those museums up there," Joy said.

"No, nowhere like that. Everything is just in the apartment right now," Constance said. At least this time she hadn't used "my apartment." "*The* apartment" betrayed no one.

"What you waiting for?" Tracy asked.

"Well, somebody's gotta want to see it," Constance said.

"You believe in you?" Gina asked. Constance nodded, afraid of chastisement if she shrugged her shoulders or told her maybe. "You got somebody else who believe in you?" Gina asked. Constance nodded, picturing Brian that night in New York, Brian insisting that all she needed was the time to become a great artist. "Then you got everything. You bring one of those in here. We'll make space on the counter or something. Move Mr. Bruce over for a few days."

"That's too sweet of you," Constance said, waving

away Gina's offer. She didn't know if they would like her work, if it might strike them as too foreign, as too little, as too much.

"You need something. We can give it to you. No museum in New York, but we can start calling that counter, the Winging It! Gallery. Might as well do it now before we can't anymore."

"What do you mean?" Constance asked. Joy and Tracy's heads were hung a bit and Mr. Bruce lowered the rim of his hat.

"We closing at the end of the month," Gina said.

***

Winging It! opened in 1968, Gina told her. She and her silent-type husband had watched DC burn after Martin Luther King's assassination. They didn't live in Shaw, where the most damage was done, but they had both grown up around H Street, which had burned almost entirely that day in April. They wanted to do something and they thought what the city needed was new black businesses, people who could show they believed in the city. They borrowed and begged from whomever they could to open and even bought the building.

"Nobody was thinking about this building, about this neighborhood. Scandal how cheap it was and now, they telling us we can get all kinds of money for it. We said no for a long time, but they get personal. They come in saying, 'Ma'am, you must want to do something else. You must not want to stand in here frying chicken for people. Who would want that?' Like my whole life don't mean a thing."

Developers were looking for areas for new condos. This section was filled with single-family homes, not as easy to rent out to young professionals who wanted shiny new amenities without the hassle of a house. The privilege of ownership.

"You can't close," Constance told her. "What will the neighborhood do?"

"Change come for all of us, honey," Gina said and sent her on her way with three free chicken wings.

But that night, welcoming change wasn't what Constance wanted to do. She ranted to Brian instead.

"More than forty years," she told him, shaking a spatula at him as vegetables sizzled in a skillet. "They started because of the riots. This is how neighborhoods are destroyed."

Brian cracked open a beer and took a seat at the kitchen table. "Well, we should go and support them as much as we can before they close."

Constance nodded, but she didn't want him coming into Winging It! with her. She didn't want them to know that she was with a white guy and that the way she talked when she was with them wasn't the way she talked when she was with him.

"Someone decides that newer is better," she said. "People have no sense of their history. And this developer she's selling to, he's done this all over the city. Put developments in historically black neighborhoods, moved out small businesses." She got two plates down from the cabinet and began to dish up a plate for him. "I'm going to email some people. Maybe the *Washington Post*, the *City Paper*, local stations, tell them the story and see if I can get something to happen." She set his plate in front of him.

"You talked to them about this?" Brian said. He began eating, furrowing his brow as he did. "They want you to stop it?"

"You haven't even been in there," Constance said. She opened a beer for herself and took a long sip. She turned away from him.

"You're right. Maybe I should go in soon."

"Don't go just because I said to go," she said, pressing reprimand into her voice so insistently that he would feel it.

"What? Who said that? And you didn't say I should go, you've never said that."

"The point is, it's a real shame," she said. Constance began to make a plate for herself.

"What's a shame is people burning their own neighborhoods. It's like, why do that?" he said.

"Rage," she said. One of her aunts had witnessed the Watts riots in '65. She had told Constance that all that love had to go somewhere. Constance had asked, "Love?" "I guess you thought that was hate?" her aunt had said.

"Of course. But in the end, rioting accomplishes nothing." He laid his hands out on the table, open in supplication.

"I don't know if protest is always meant to be productive," she said. "Sometimes you just have to get something out of your system."

"Only to destroy yourself?"

★★★

Television coverage was more than Constance expected, but the call to the *City Paper* had yielded interest. The reporter there had mentioned a reporter he knew at a local station. That reporter called Constance and said they could do a live remote the next day. Constance put on a bright orange dress, something vivid for the cameras, and got there just before noon.

"Anne won't come out," the reporter said to Constance after a brief hello and handshake. Constance turned to Winging It! and back to the reporter, doused in perfume and the irritation of someone with something better to do.

"Anne?"

"The owner." The reporter began to reek of her indignation. "She says she's running her business and doesn't have time for some news story."

"Well, it is the lunch rush." Inside Winging It!, the crowd was dense, hungry patrons layered over one another. Constance couldn't find Gina/Anne in all of that thickness. "Maybe after, you could talk to her," Constance offered.

"It's a live remote. I told you. You're gonna have to talk."

Constance craned again to see if she could spot Gina. She saw Tracy yelling over her shoulder, probably at Earl for an order. Constance couldn't catch her eye and going inside to talk to one of them felt pointless, casting her voice on too turbulent a sea. "Okay," she said.

Constance dabbed a tissue at her nose and cheekbones, hoping to clear any shine that the camera might catch. The cameraman counted them down to go live. The reporter struck a smile, her teeth shining brightly, and thanked the anchor miles away in the studio. Constance tried to construct sentences in her head to make sure she wouldn't fumble any words, but the reporter's intro was too short and the microphone was in her face too soon.

"And how long have you been coming to Winging It!?" the reporter asked.

"Forever it feels like," Constance said. Two times seemed an infinitesimal number to tell her. "Gina and the girls have made it feel like home." Constance had used her private name, but there was no recovery on live television.

"And what makes the food so good?"

"Well, it's the best fried chicken in the city," Constance parroted Mr. Bruce's pronouncement since she hadn't had fried chicken from anywhere else. "And of course, you have to get it with the mambo sauce."

"And what makes this place important?"

"It's a cornerstone of the community and when we allow developers to come in and take away these cornerstones, the whole structure collapses. This developer has done this all over DC and here's a place where we can take a stand against it. They think they know better than the people of this community what is best for them. We think they're wrong."

The reporter moved the mic away. "The developer has suggested a mixed-use complex, some condos as well as retail. But inside right now, lots of hungry Washingtonians are getting their fill of this institution before it closes. Anna Bruce and her husband, George, started this restaurant in the wake of the riots of 1968, and now this city will be losing a place to all sit down at the table of brotherhood as Dr. King would have said, with some of the best fried chicken in the city in hand."

The cameraman swung toward the door of Winging It! just as Brian exited, a greasy white paper bag in his hands, Gina behind him.

"Back to you."

★★★

Gina had beckoned Constance into Winging It! with just one wave of her hand and one set, stern line of her mouth. Constance asked Brian to wait outside, she wouldn't be long, she said. Brian followed her back inside anyway, as if the words she'd spoken had been no more than her own discarded thought. She tried to stand just a bit apart from Brian. Not that she was denying him or that they were together; she wouldn't do that. She just wanted to handle her own business with Gina, explain that it was like Gina had told her about bringing in a sculpture: they had needed something and Constance had been able to give it.

"Who asked you to do that?" Gina asked. Her hands rushed the air, propelled by anger toward Constance and the sidewalk that the news crew had abandoned only minutes ago. Constance opened her mouth to reply, but stopped. "You know my name?" Gina said. "Or hers?" She pointed at Tracy. "So, how you know what I want?"

"I just thought if you could stay here," Constance's voice began to rise, "it would be better," she said.

"For you?" Gina said. "So you can come in here and chat with women who work for a living?"

"I told you, I sculpt," Constance said quietly.

"And live with your white boyfriend," Gina said. Constance looked around Winging It!, but Mr. Bruce wouldn't meet her eyes and neither would any of the other women. "That's your man, sister?" Gina asked. She pointed her finger at Constance, her ordering finger, the one that gave you permission to ask for what you were willing to pay for, the one that allowed her to give you what you were looking for or tell you that they were all out of that.

"It's been six months," she said. Constance shrank inside, her courage fleeting enough to escape her in one short sneeze.

Gina lowered her finger and shook her head. "You think just because you black, you not changing this neighborhood?" she said. Constance's hand went to her hair, feeling for her blackness. Gina raised her finger again, this time for Brian. "He asked questions. Wanted me to tell him what was the best choice, how he should order, whether people really got salt, pepper, and hot sauce or if that would make it too salty. You came in here like you knew. You never asked anything. You thought you knew better. You thought you *were* better. Just because you live on this side of town don't mean you don't think like they do on the other side of town. Go save a business in Georgetown, honey," she said, punctuating the most important words with her finger. That finger ruled the whole place.

"I was helping."

"You were interfering. I knew who I was selling this place to. Maybe that developer puts a good grocery store in here or a drugstore that doesn't keep its soap under lock and key. I love this place, put my whole life into even the corners of it, but even I know there are better things in this world than two-dollar fried chicken wings." She pointed one red nail to the plateglass window and the gray of the neighborhood beyond it. "But you too busy knowing it all to ever figure out what someone else knows. You so sure of things, how come you didn't know to tell us you didn't move down here alone?" Gina thumbed in Brian's direction. "Now, I gotta hope this developer don't say to me, 'Never mind,' don't say, 'Maybe she's too much trouble to sell to and maybe those Chinese down the street might be easier to deal with.' Now, I gotta make sure that the life I decided I wanted isn't gonna get wrecked by some girl who don't even know what the hell my name is."

Gina slammed a fist onto the counter. She turned

and walked through the doors to the back. Constance and the whole room watched her go. Then the others turned to Constance. She headed straight for the door, Brian stood still behind her. His face was filled with the fire that had just been on Gina's. Before she could reach the door, she caught her foot on Mr. Bruce's cane. He didn't give her any of his teasing, none of his innuendo. She was quiet too, begging in silence to just get out of the door. Outside, shame and the smell of grease clung to her.

* * *

Brian eventually came outside and began to walk to their house, in front of Constance. Her feet didn't bother to catch up, unsure of how deep the water was around her and with no insurance to take care of the damage after. In their apartment, Brian was hushed. The rustle of the bag from Winging It! when he set it down with no gentleness, with no ease, was the loudest of anything.

"Why didn't they know about me?" he asked.

Constance didn't know what answer would be both true and painless. She could find none.

"She made it sound like I was hiding something," she said.

"You never said, 'My boyfriend thinks' or 'My boyfriend says'?"

"I didn't talk to them like that."

"It's only been six months, right?"

"I was helping. I was doing my best."

"People are always lying when they say that."

"You don't understand anything," she said, but tried to bury the words in an exhale.

"Say that again," he said. Constance could not and she still could not look at him.

"No, I understand everything," he said. He walked away from her.

Before long, the apartment began to darken. Constance went into the kitchen, wanting a beer or perhaps nothing at all. The chicken, still in its white bag, sat on the table, cold and neglected. It seemed a shame for it to be wasted, but Constance thought it best to get it out of the house. She would have scrubbed her memory of this afternoon if she could have, at least she could scrub the kitchen of it. She pushed the bag into the trash, ripping it as she did. Mambo sauce tumbled out and when she pushed more, the small plastic containers opened. Dark sauce spilled on its journey to the bottom of the bin. Maybe she had never even liked the taste of mambo sauce. The vinegar too sharp and the sweetness too thick. She hadn't been tasting the sauce as much as she had been tasting newness. That was what those developers wanted.

Gentrification was always good at first: fresher produce at the grocery store, a cleaner subway station. Then, a new shop replaced the family-owned one that had been there for decades. The crumbling row house—an eyesore for its boarded-up windows, but beautiful when the first snow collected in the jagged remnants of its roof—is gone one day to make way for high-rise condos.

This is what Brian didn't understand: once gentrification started it could not be stopped. And Constance was afraid love would do the same to her.

TRAINING SCHOOL FOR NEGRO GIRLS

Janice had never been a dancer in a rap video, but she could have been. Sure, in her kitchen right now, it doesn't seem possible. She's only a B cup and the visible belly bulge from the domestic life of a husband and two kids is destroying all illusions. She isn't oiled down and no one in her home is popping bottles. But trust, she's about to bring it. See that hip pop? What she wants to do is kick off those driving moccasins because she has every reason to whip and Nae Nae.

After a month, Shelby has finally called. Shelby, the queen bee of the Washington black middle class. Shelby, Janice's machete in the battle for class domination.

And now, she could walk into her living room, pitch her voice to its zenith, and say to her husband, Nathan, "Well! You will never believe who that was!"

Playing games was best for them both. The marriage was in its tenth year and their conversations had become ordinary. She was left to make her voice shrill and gesture in large arcs. All he gave in return was a mono-tone voice and the same raised eyebrows. She made the holiday dinners; she also had to make the excitement.

The phone call from Shelby would set some things right in their life. Toby & Tiffany events would bring new energy to their lives. The kids would meet other children of their caliber, actually better caliber. Their daughter, Andrea, was cute enough once Janice decorated her with elaborate ribbons and bows, sometimes both togeth-er on her overlarge head. The space from Andrea's eye-brows to the crown of her watermelon-shaped dome was a vast amount of real estate. Paul, their son, was more acceptable to Janice. He wasn't good-looking—Janice had married Nathan more for his planned ascension at a DC public relations firm than for his looks—but he was inoffensive and six. His head was more cantaloupe then watermelon.

Toby & Tiffany would give her and Nathan endless nights filled with conversations of black middle class striving. Toby & Tiffany was the first step to that kind of happiness. The organization didn't accept applica-tions: you had to be sponsored by two other members. Or you had to be a legacy, the latest generation of college-educated "New Negroes" who wanted to spend time with other college-educated New Negroes. Shelby wanted to have lunch and the conversation could only be about sponsorship.

Black Washingtonians drag raced their classic Mercedes-Benzes through the streets, let their newly pressed hair hang out of the window on their way to a friend's Kwanzaa gathering in PG County. Janice could feel the wind right now, and although she didn't yet have a friend in a suburb like Prince George's County—although the black middle class flight had been happening for decades—she would find one, sort through the undesirables out there to instead find the ones who lived in better areas. Pour out the Olde English and stock up on the Johnnie Walker Black!

★★★

At a hundred-dollar-a-plate dinner a month ago, Janice and Nathan were at a table with Shelby and her husband, Everett. The talk among the ten seated with them turned to education, and both Janice and Shelby made reference to their college years "back East" at a "prestigious" university with a "storied" list of alumnae. This went on all night, until someone said, "Shit. Which Ivy? Just damn well say it."

Janice and Shelby went to clutch their pearls at the same time, and Janice knew she had found a kindred spirit. The man who had verbally accosted them had of course not gone to an Ivy or one of the three good HBCUs. Apparently, he had attended a state school. Not even the fact that he was deputy director of the Department of Energy could erase that kind of shame. Why was Obama letting these people in? He'd gone to an Ivy.

They quickly forgot he had even opened his mouth what with all their reminiscing, the clubs they belonged to, spring breaks on the Vineyard, and of course, which sorority they pledged. They hand signaled and called to each other from two seats away when the other wanted more bread and butter. Janice nearly choked on her baguette when Shelby mentioned T&T.

"TNT?" Nathan said. He laughed. "You talking about dynamite or about the channel?"

Janice whacked him on his knee under the table.

Shelby leaned in to them, casting a dark eye toward Mr. and Mrs. State School. "T&T is Toby & Tiffany."

"Of course," Janice said. Her heart hammered into her strapless bra. She didn't know if it was the waist cincher or the revelation that Shelby was a member of Toby & Tiffany, but Janice couldn't breathe.

"You two are totally T&T material," Shelby said. She tapped Everett on his shoulder and he bobbled his head. "The last selection season was abysmal."

Janice lurched forward and thought she heard the zipper on her dress break.

"We had—God—plumbers and police officers and," Shelby paused to lower her voice, "kindergarten teachers." She threw her hands and waved her fingers as though kindergarten teachers were so much debris in the air.

Everett bobbled again, but this time Janice thought she felt a hand on her knee nearest him. Janice looked down and Everett looked away.

"I called a meeting of T&T parents and said, 'Look, if you can't bring quality people in here then maybe you're not quality and maybe you,' you know, meaning them, 'maybe you, shouldn't be in T&T either.'" Shelby sat back and crossed her arms, as satisfied now as she had been with that proposition then.

Janice hurried to fill the silence with praise, something effusive, but meaningful: "Wow. You go girl." She deflated as soon as the phrase left her mouth. Damn. This wasn't 1992, or even 2002 if she were white and ten years behind the curve.

But apparently, Shelby liked both those bygone eras.

"Exactly," she said. "Exactly. I go. I"—she pressed a finger into her décolletage—"go." She threw her hand out to the table at the word and nodded to her new chant.

Janice smiled and bobbled even better than Everett.

"You should be a T&T'er," Shelby said. "Give me your number."

***

Shelby suggested Old Ebbitt Grill for lunch, right around the corner from the White House and often the site of high-powered Washington lunches. Janice eased into a green velvet booth across from Shelby when she arrived. Shelby leaned toward her, but didn't even bother to fake a kiss.

"And no need to apologize for being late," she said. She patted Janice's hand. Janice didn't want to check her watch, but she was sure that when she last looked at her cell phone on the way in she was ten minutes early.

"Right," Janice said. "Sorry about that."

"Where are you coming from again?" she asked. Janice didn't think Shelby had ever known at all.

"Northeast," Janice said.

"Oh. People say there are some nice houses there," Shelby said with deliberateness. "I wouldn't know. I've never been outside Northwest except of course to go to Northern Virginia, Montgomery County, or PG County. I don't even drive through those neighborhoods to get to Maryland or Virginia."

"But PG is right by Northeast."

"Right," Shelby said. She unfolded her napkin as she nodded. "I just take the Beltway around the city, so I can avoid it."

"Makes sense," Janice said. No, it didn't, but if T&T made her swear a blood oath to never leave Northwest, she would do it. They could move. The kids could transfer schools. She could quit her job.

"Ladies," the waiter said. He poured both of them full glasses of water.

"I'd love lemon in mine," Janice said. He nodded.

"Cucumber," Shelby said. The waiter nodded, but slowly, and Shelby repeated the word. She started making small circles in the air, the shape, Janice supposed, of cucumber slices. It looked instead like the hand motion for crazy that had lost its way on the journey to the side of her head. Actually, crazy probably should be wild, random hand motions. Shelby was on to something. The waiter turned to Janice for translation.

"Cucumber" was all Janice managed. Shelby began pointing with vigor at Janice. "I think she wants cucumber for her water," Janice said. "If you have it of course."

"And also a bottle of Chablis and the soft-shell crab."

The waiter nodded and began backing away from the

insufferable game of charades. When he returned shortly after, he offered the plate of cucumbers to Shelby like a virgin hoping to avoid the volcano.

"Our parents," Shelby began, "Everett's and mine." Shelby paused to sip her cucumber water and Janice briefly considered that they might be sibling spouses. The royals had married within their families, no one could tell the black upper class of Washington they couldn't do the same. If incest was good enough for white people, it was good enough for them. "We are legacies you see. Both of us. Love that was fated." Shelby smiled, her face soft in remembrance. "You see, I wasn't supposed to be at the No to Naps benefit. Incredible organization really, they raise money for underprivileged black children who cannot afford relaxers. Not just the girls either." Shelby shook her relaxed hair in rapid defiance. "They also raise money for the boys, for texturizers of course. They won't stop until they've eradicated natural hair. These children in the hood in those dreadlocks." Shelby's eyes doubled in size like the stabbing in a horror movie had just flashed before her eyes. "Have you seen them? No one is talking about this tragedy that's happening in our communities." Shelby emphasized her words by tapping her French-manicured index finger onto the white tablecloth. "Once we were a people who never wore our hair natural. We've forgotten who we are."

Janice nodded solemnly. She didn't think every kid needed straightened hair, she'd waited until this year to put a baby perm in Andrea's hair. Fourth grade was clearly the right time to be kink free. Their food arrived, salad for Janice and the soft-shell crab for Shelby.

"You see, that's why Toby & Tiffany is so important," Shelby said.

For the eradication of naps? Janice didn't want to play this wrong after the "You go girl" incident.

"Family," Shelby provided instead.

"Yes, absolutely," Janice agreed. "That's why I, well Nathan and I, are so excited about the possibility of joining you all. For the good of our family."

"One day Janice, your little girl . . ." Shelby stopped to puzzle. "You do have a little girl, right?"

"And a boy," Janice said.

"Your own little Toby and Tiffany." Shelby tilted her head as if looking at puppies in a window who had flopped over onto their backs. "Everett and I just have a Tiffany. We're both onlies and when you have more than one child, they suffer." Shelby spread her hands out toward Janice in confirmation. "No, Toby, you can't go to Paris with us because the cost of your ticket is our wine budget. No, Toby, you can't go to college because Daddy wants a golf course in the backyard. You know?" Shelby said.

Janice considered this thinking. Didn't you, though, have to give yourself a backup plan if one of your kids ended up with a nasty crack habit? Or meth? Did black people do meth? Or were black people still doing crack? She hadn't been keeping up.

"I just don't want to say no to my child. Anyway, one day your little Tiffany might find out that her perfect

Toby has been her playmate since they were children. She'll know he's quality and that together they can backstab to get to the top. Kismet, I think they call it."

"Sounds like it," Janice said. "Sounds perfect."

"Your little girl's little girl can be a legacy one day, a double legacy. It's what we work for. It's what our ancestors died for. What those protestors marched in . . ." Shelby paused. "Was it Alabama?" She couldn't locate the answer. "Somewhere in the South for," she finished her speech.

Janice was sold. It was what she'd been working toward. She would get to the mountaintop; they as a family would get to the mountaintop. Her heart began to hum "We Shall Overcome."

"I have to get back to Northwest," Shelby said.

"We are in Northwest," Janice said, and then tempered her know-it-all-ness. "Aren't we?"

"My part of Northwest," she said. "I can't stay Downtown for long. This part of Northwest still feels a little seedy to me. The monuments and museums. No thank you." Shelby made a check mark in the air to their waiter.

Janice took out her card, prepared to pay her half.

"I don't know if they take AmEx," Shelby said. The waiter walked over. "Do you take that?" She pointed down at Janice's card.

"Oh yes," he said.

"Great." She smiled. "Go on and settle our bill then." The waiter reached down for Janice's card and although her impulse was to smack his hand or play some form of keep-away, she did neither. Instead, she smiled at Shelby who burped softly before moving her linen napkin in front of her face. "Asparagus," she said.

***

Janice was pissed about Shelby sticking her with the bill, but it must be some T&T test. If you had enough money to not look at bills, you must be financially well-off enough to get in. Tonight mattered more to seal their sponsorship: a T&T parent mixer at a member's home in, of course, Northwest.

Nathan looked nice. He knew how to dress well from all his client meetings, and before they walked out the door to the sounds of a panda movie the babysitter put on, Janice determined that they looked damn good together.

The house for the mixer was white with columns and a brick walkway. The walk wended to the columned front. The front yard was well manicured, the lawn looked to be all the same height. Janice could see all the smallest details because the owners had installed searching movie-premiere lights.

"Is that a diamond-ring topiary?" Janice asked Nathan.

He lifted his eyebrows and monotoned, "Looks like it."

From behind the band of the ring came a small Latino man. He was probably Salvadoran or Guatemalan. Mexicans didn't often make their way to DC, and Shelby told her she was glad for that. "We get the exotic Hispanics. Don't you think *Hua-te-mala* sounds better than *May-he-co*?"

A Hua-te-malan woman greeted them at the door with a tray of champagne glasses. Janice thanked her once and then again feeling a twinge of pity for her and her countryman outside. But the champagne was good, and what would they do without her there? Get champagne themselves?

Shelby spotted them shortly thereafter and walked them both around the party that was just beginning to fill up. The names and faces blurred because they all looked so much alike, fair to tan in color, shoulder-length relaxed hair or closely cropped haircuts with names that bounced happily from syllable to syllable. I'm *Dun*-dun and this is Dun-*dun*. Janice strained to subvert the monotony, but when she told them her and Nathan's names it sounded just like all the other introductions. The first hour was almost all introductions and brief, mostly awkward conversations. Janice and Nathan found a seat to get a little peace.

Then, they started playing hip hop in the second hour. Janice poked Nathan. "See, no more adult contemporary," she said.

Nathan scrunched up his face. "Is this the theme song from that nineties movie where the white teacher goes and saves inner-city children?"

Janice listened. "Yeah, but not the first one, the sequel where she had to go back to the inner city to save them because when she left they let it all go to shit again."

Nathan hit her on the leg in the excitement of recognition. "Right, *Criminal Brains 2: A Rainbow in the Hood*."

Janice moved her shoulders in time to the music. A new song came on, more hip hop. A couple of suited men on the floor threw their hands in the air.

"This is white people hip hop," Nathan said. She covered his mouth after he said it, but when she saw the champagne tray coming by she took her hand away to grab one and down the last of the glass she already held.

"Relax. This is fun," she said. Shoulder shake. Shoulder shake. Shoulder shake.

"'This Is How We Do It'? Definitely white people hip hop." Nathan reclined on the velvet chaise lounge and widened his legs.

"Are you going into your hardcore rap stance?" Janice said.

"Compared to these dudes, when I walked in I was in my hardcore rap stance," Nathan said. "I mean come on, that guy over there? Why do you like these people?"

Janice was annoyed. He could never enjoy the things she enjoyed. "Why? Because at least we're not just sitting around the house watching some terrible movie you picked." She stood up. "I'll be back." Janice wobbled a bit on her heels, but she managed to get almost across the room when she felt a tap on her bare shoulder. Shelby smiled when Janice turned around.

"How is it?" Shelby asked.

"Great," Janice said. "Just really so very great." Janice sipped and smiled at the same time.

"I think you'll fit in nicely," Shelby put her hand back

on Janice's shoulder. "You and Nathan aren't going to dance?" The dance floor was mostly empty, but Everett was taking up enough space with turns and pseudo-break dancing for four people.

"Nathan's pretty tired."

"Well, I can't stop Everett from getting out there. He loves to wiggle it." Shelby pulled Janice closer to her. "He's a very special man you know."

"I can see that," Janice said. She was jealous of Shelby, how her face had glowed when she talked about Everett at lunch, how now her voice danced to his beat, no matter how off tempo it was.

Shelby turned to face Janice. "He's very light skinned," Shelby confided. "It's a blessing." She turned her attention back to Everett and tilted her head in admiration. Nathan was certainly not very light skinned. Janice grew even more annoyed at him.

"He's so high up in Homeland Security, I don't even know what he does," Shelby said. "You don't know what your husband does, do you?"

Janice choked on her champagne. She could feel a hive developing on her cheek. She might be getting drunk or, more likely, the acute embarrassment of knowing not only Nathan's title but the acronym for the office supply requisition form and what pastries Marie, the office manager, ordered for their morning staff meeting.

Everett walked toward them, wiping sweat from his forehead. Shelby took her hand away from Janice and wrapped an arm around Everett. He began thrusting into Shelby's thigh, concentration etched onto his face.

"He's a wild one," Shelby said, swatting his thrusts away. The host T&T'er had some emergency, something about the caterer running out of arugula bites and offering to substitute fried collard greens, and she pulled Shelby away.

Everett thrusted in the air to the music. Over his shoulder, Janice saw Nathan sitting by himself. He indeed wasn't very light skinned, but Janice decided maybe that wasn't a bad thing.

"You want to see my car?" Everett asked. "It's outside and it's hot in here." Everett liking her was just as important as Shelby liking her. He was drunk, but she might be too, maybe the air would help.

"Sure."

"Out this way," he instructed.

The place was larger than Janice realized, but in the darkened hallway she couldn't tell if they were passing bedrooms or storage closets. Everett knew though. He thrust into Janice's back so forcefully that she tumbled into one of the dark spaces. She dropped her champagne, but it fell noiselessly onto the carpet.

Everett pulled her in, grabbing her ass. Janice's mouth gaped. Everett was a tangle of grabby and thrusting limbs.

"You're so," Everett searched for the word, "black. It's so refreshing. I bet you don't even try to lighten your skin." He moved closer to her. "Am I right?" He moved to bury his nose in the crook of her neck. "Am I right?"

Janice smelled texturizer, apparently Everett was also saying No to Naps.

"Uh, maybe you shouldn't do that. What if Shelby were to walk—" Janice stopped when a light turned on. Shelby. If only Janice could use that clairvoyance for good. Everett let her go and Janice took a step away from him in what she could now see was a bedroom. *Nice duvet cover*, Janice thought.

"Everett," Shelby reprimanded.

"Shelby," Janice began, "he's drunk and I think he probably even thought I was you." Janice hoped that lie would help.

Shelby folded her arms and stared Everett down.

"It was a mistake," Janice said quietly. "We all make them."

Everett walked out of the bedroom, but Janice stayed, unsure if under all that poised veneer was a girl who loved nothing more than a catfight. Shelby began to walk out after Everett, but turned back at the last minute.

"I don't blame you," Shelby said. "Not much anyway."

***

Janice called Shelby multiple times over the next week to say how sorry she was and to say that she hoped this wouldn't threaten their future relationship. She didn't want to say T&T, but she hoped Shelby knew that by future she meant more T&T mixers where she would stay far away from Everett. Every time the calls had gone to voice mail, but finally Shelby texted her, "Coffee shop, 14th and T, 5pm." Shelby had needed time to get over the shock of seeing her husband with his face in another woman's neck. She was sure Shelby had talked seriously with Everett, and was now firm on the pronouncement she'd made to Janice that night: she wasn't to blame.

Inside the coffee shop, Shelby was in a corner with a large mug already in front of her.

"Shelby," Janice started.

Shelby held up her hand. "You've apologized. A lot. Twenty voice mails I had to delete," she said.

"I just wanted you to know that I was genuinely sorry."

"I know that." Shelby sighed. "I do."

"Good, I wouldn't want to lose you as a friend."

Shelby twirled her mug around on the tabletop. "Are we friends?"

"I thought so. I thought that's part of what T&T was about. Friends. Family."

"No, I said it was about family."

"Right, well. Aren't the T&T folks almost like family?"

Shelby considered this. "I guess, maybe like the Corleones. Like how Michael killed Fredo on the lake that time. Or when Michael has Connie's husband killed. A family that betrays you."

Janice didn't respond. She'd said *husband*, *betray*, and *kill*. Best not to encourage that line of thinking.

Shelby picked up her mug with both hands and took a drink. "It doesn't appear that you'll be joining our little organization," Shelby said. She shrugged her shoulders and then wiped chai-tea foam from her upper lip. "Maybe next year."

Janice knew that was a lie, an imaginary carrot. Or canapé, that felt more class appropriate, something that

174

Shelby would order for her MLK champagne brunch. An imaginary canapé. Anyway, it wasn't the truth. She wasn't going to get in and she knew Shelby's handsy husband was the reason.

Janice wanted to channel all her blackness and go in on this chick. She could use the black-girl voice she pulled out sometimes when race solidarity was necessary, if the meter maid was black, if the waitress was black, if the bartender could put a little more love into her vodka cranberry. She could not use her white-girl voice. That sort of perkiness wouldn't play when you needed to give somebody a good cuss out.

"Bitch." That was about right. *Deal with it Shelby*, Janice thought. She considered standing up and moving in closer to Shelby. "What?" her body language would say. Nathan did postures like that when he played dominoes or spades with his family in Georgia. She once saw him take his shoe off and put his foot on the card table, but Janice had not gone for her weekly pedicure and she knew the toenail polish in her driving moccasin was a bit chipped. She loosened up her shoulders instead, and cracked her neck just in case something popped off in the Mocha Latte Café.

"Did you say something?" Shelby asked.

Oh, okay, thought Janice. Who knew Shelby had a little street in her, that underneath that French liquid foundation there roared a tigress who wouldn't extract her claws? Wait, maybe tigers always had their claws out. Right! Just like Shelby, always just sitting there, lying in wait with her claws ready to rip into you.

"You heard me," Janice finally fired back.

"No, I didn't. What did you say?" Janice realized Shelby wasn't asking this as a challenge, as if to confirm that the word Janice said was indeed *bitch*. Shelby hadn't heard her. Janice wanted to get her courage back up. She wanted to call Shelby that word again, a word she deserved to hear. Janice, though, had used up the small crumb of courage she had on that attempt. Besides, she didn't want to play games with Shelby. She would not act as though they were on the playground. Instead, she stood up.

"No, I didn't say anything," Janice began. She turned and started for the door. "Oh wait, I just remembered: I called you a bitch." Janice didn't see Shelby's reaction because she was too determined in her run for the door. Those driving moccasins weren't just for driving.

***

Janice pulled in front of their house and sat. She didn't know whether to be sad or relieved. They would never be in T&T now, Shelby and her legacy children would see to that. When Janice finally walked into the house, she called out to Nathan, but he didn't answer. Instead, she heard a scamper of feet. Andrea came running in and barreled into Janice's middle.

"Hi Mom," Andrea said, with a lightness in her voice Janice needed to hear. "Mrs. Baker saw you drive up, so she said I could come back home."

"Why were you over there? Daddy and Paul aren't

here?" Janice asked, leading her daughter over to the living room couch.

"They went to get dinner," she said. "Daddy thought you wouldn't want to cook."

"Daddy was right," Janice said. Her daughter had such a sweetness about her. She smiled often, but it was more than that. Light seemed to beam from her every pore. She didn't look for things to make her happy, she woke up that way and managed to stay that way all day long. It was a skill Janice wondered if she'd had as a child, but lost in the midst of career and marriage and social climbing. She needed to be more like Andrea. Janice reached up and took off the beribboned headband she'd put on Andrea that morning. She reached out to her little girl's chin and tilted her face up, but then the light bounced off her forehead and Janice quickly put the headband back on Andrea's enormous head.

NOW, THIS

Inadequacies and too-bright Christmas lights were on crass and pleasing display at the Windows and Walls office Christmas party. Last year, at a lavish Downtown DC restaurant, the food had been unpronounceable. This year, buckets of chicken on break-room counters doubled as centerpieces, cut poinsettias lay lopsided atop the drumsticks. Next year, Rae was sure there would be one mini cupcake with a candy cane wedged into the icing on their desks at five.

Everyone was taking what they could get.

Maggie, her twenty-seven-year-old supervisor, had once taken the opportunity to tell Rae that she wanted to look like her when she was over forty. Perhaps Maggie would exchange her long, blond hair for Rae's full, picked-out fro right around thirty-five. Marcus, Rae's cubicle-mate, was taking the dance floor by storm, voguing to a teen pop song. Not many straight brothers vogued.

"He's a good dancer," Maggie said. Rae gifted her with a noncommittal nod.

Now was an ideal time for a drink, but no alcohol had accompanied the chicken.

In her twenties after a night of drinking, Rae would cry, a trail of clothes from the front door to the bathroom the only witness. She would look in the mirror after vomiting and think how different she was going to make her life—as soon as she brushed her teeth.

She was already making better choices, the relationship with Homeland Security was over. He, the king of the jackasses. He, also, of the penis the size of a portly child's arm. But, when Rae felt a wetness between her legs watching Marcus—small-child-attacking-a-birthday-piñata-eager Marcus—somehow, she wasn't surprised. She was ready to move on.

Then, the wetness ran, spread. She sat to contain the moisture, but the shifting didn't stop it. Maybe her period had arrived. She didn't keep track. She never bothered to figure out if the twenty-eight-day cycle was from the first day of one period to the next or from the first of one to the last of the other. When the gap between her periods widened—not unlike her ass—she could never confirm it. Her attention was elsewhere: her mother's doctor's appointments or the soul-killing work of copywriting. She stood to cross the room to the door with the gold LADIES sign on it. Maggie put a hand on her back.

"You have a wet spot on your skirt. You must have sat in water," she whispered.

In the stall, Rae discovered it wasn't water and it wasn't blood. The crotch of her panties was soaked, but this wetness wasn't an urge for pleasure. Her panties were wet with urine.

***

Parenting magazines cluttered the glass table in the reception area of Dr. Sapna's office. Rae thumbed her phone screen instead. The elderly office manager was making an appointment for a woman at the desk, broadcasting her need to get an ultrasound for her fibroids. Good thing the girl didn't have scabies. A young Asian woman came in. Worry ran a lap around her face and her hands touched her protruding stomach. The nurse called Rae's name. She considered giving the young woman a reassuring phrase as they passed, but resisted when all Rae could think of was: *Good luck with that.*

The nurse took her vitals and once alone, Rae removed her winter layers. She wrapped the paper gown around her to keep out the room's chill and sat on the exam table. The Pap smear had been scheduled for months, but now there was the urination problem last week, the acne, the erratic periods.

"You ready?" Dr. Sapna asked from outside the exam room after Rae had watched one too many internet videos on her phone to pass the time.

"Ready." Rae dismissed a text from her mother, really

her mother's home health aide. A text from her mother would have included nonsensical emoticons instead of the single letters and numbers of the young aide. "When r u going 2 b home?"

Dr. Sapna entered, brown, beautiful, also single. "Shall we?"

Rae obliged and reclined.

"How's that guy you were dating last time?" Dr. Sapna asked. She pulled back the front of Rae's gown and began kneading her breasts as if written across them was "Bake at 350° for 20–30 minutes."

"That's all done," Rae said.

"What did he do?"

"We just weren't the people for each other."

"Oh. So, he ended it." Dr. Sapna stopped her baking preparations and closed the front of Rae's gown. "Well, now all you need to do is get over it. We don't have time to waste, do we? Slide down, legs open."

Rae drew the front of her gown together. Dr. Sapna had already seen everything, but the lights were on and Rae was ashamed of what they were about to do.

"No need for a refill on the birth control?"

"No."

Dr. Sapna nodded from in between Rae's legs. "Huh, your cervix points straight up."

"Is that normal?" Rae asked. She craned to see the answer in Dr. Sapna's face, but the top of her head didn't have much expression.

She swabbed Rae and stood up. "Normal is relative with our bodies. There's a range."

"Right." Sexual partners had commented on the size of her areolas or the shade of pink of her labia. The next time she was naked with someone, critiques would not be welcome.

"Two weeks for the results. Anything else?" Dr. Sapna asked.

Rae slipped her feet out of the faux fur–covered stirrups and sat up. She gave each concern to Dr. Sapna, but she didn't take them bit by bit. She took them all, timber or twig, and damn well started a fire.

Rae could not remember her mother talking about perimenopause, which Rae first thought was the stage before premenopause. Pre-premenopause.

"No," Dr. Sapna told her. "Just one stop before you hit menopause." Rae imagined her vagina as a train making station stops. Surely it would be one of those environmentally unfriendly locomotives, not a sleek bullet train. For that, of course, she would have had to be shaved. "The journey there could take years. Or . . ."

"Or?" Rae pressed.

"It could be months. How long have your periods been erratic?" Dr. Sapna asked, poised with a pen to record the answer.

"A year, I guess," Rae said. She stopped. "Maybe two."

"Well, two years would tell us that menopause isn't far off. We won't know how your body adapts to this time in your fertility cycle," Dr. Sapna said.

"My infertility cycle?" Rae joked. She ripped at the paper under her thighs.

"You could still have time." She patted Rae on an

exposed knee. "I froze my eggs. There's in vitro. Adoption. Or, maybe you don't even want a family."

* * *

The lights in the aisle of the drugstore near Dr. Sapna's office were as bright as those in the examination room, but these corners had displays of age-defying makeup and not plastic containers for sharp instruments. Visits to both were necessary, but the drugstore was cheaper and less invasive. Maybe she was out of lotion. Maybe it was time for a mascara that would deliver fuller lashes. Maybe she needed a cart.

She wended a path down aisle after aisle, until aisle five. Deep pink, green, and blue plastic packages of pads and tampons sat unsympathetic. Since she was twelve, at least once a month she had needed to think about what it meant to be a woman. Rae still didn't have the answer. The last of her girlfriends to get her period, now the only of her girlfriends to have always had her period. For years, Rae's body had been preparing for an event that had never occurred.

All dressed up with no child to grow.

The opposite side of the aisle could testify: baby bottles, bibs, and diapers in lighter shades than the pads and tampons. A couple of her friends had married and had babies. Others had decided to go it alone when the clang of their clocks had drowned out the voices of cultural derision. Then, there were the friends who had gotten pregnant only to miscarry or abort. Rae didn't know the emptiness of either of those losses, one by fate, the other by fated choice. At least their wombs had known a life.

Maybe she didn't even want a family.

On a package of infant diapers, a brown baby gurgled. He stared, waiting for her to change his poopy diaper and tell him in low, soft tones that she was there, right there. She grabbed at his face and put the package in her cart. Someone should take him home.

But, those weren't the diapers she really needed.

Her mother's broken hip had declared that Rae move out of her apartment in Dupont Circle and into her childhood home in Brightwood. The doctor had recited statistics, the high possibility of breaking the hip again and the increased likelihood of death in the first year. Then, at the rehabilitation clinic, they noticed problems with her right hand's strength. A minor stroke that could have happened years before. More statistics about death. It would have been inappropriate to ask the doctor a third time if she really needed to move in.

She took one package of adult diapers off the shelf, the ones her mother insisted she get: for light incontinence. "I only pee a little," her mother confided with pride. The plastic landed with a gentle thud on the metal latticework of the cart.

A woman could live only in this aisle, picking from one side and then the other. Fertile and single, a mother, an old lady. Womanhood was a tiny endeavor according to the designers of drugstores.

Rae hurtled the cart forward. The adult diapers lurched from one end of the basket to the other. She should buy at least one more pack for her mother. She reached out for another soft package. That one bounced onto the first and then onto the metal. They were two kinds, one for maximum protection, one for lighter days. But there were also fashion colors and one with removable tabs. She pulled them both down from the shelf into her basket. And then, she pulled a whole row down and they tumbled onto each other. The basket couldn't contain a couple of them and those she held under one arm and with the other pushed the filled cart to the checkout.

The cashier looked at the Everest of adult diapers. "Are these on special?"

"My mother needs them," Rae said. "She has trouble with . . . this." She gestured to the packages.

The cashier smiled. "Do you have a club card?"

Rae fished for it while the cashier scanned and bagged her purchases.

"Did you mean to get this too?" The cashier held up the Pampers.

"Yes," Rae said. Somewhere an Amber Alert was going off: a childless forty-one-year-old woman buying baby diapers.

She hurried to swipe and sign for it all without even hearing the total. She pushed her bags and bags of adult diapers out of the store, but the cashier stopped her.

"You have a coupon printing," she said. "Looks like it's two dollars off," she paused as she read the small rectangular strip of paper, "a bedpan."

"Thanks, who can ever have enough bedpans?"

For the majority of her adult life, Rae had consumed her meals standing at the stove or she had eaten peanut butter from the jar. Now, Rae and her mother ate dinner (never peanut butter, nothing straight from a jar) in front of the television in the living room. It was the closest room to the converted back bedroom. Her mother couldn't walk unassisted. The cane wasn't enough and after a while her arms ached from the walker. The row house hadn't been intended for a wheelchair and even her mother's two legs plus the walker's four was a squeeze. Her mother took her time, the way she did anything now, to make the steps from her bedroom. Then, she sat, breathing heavily from the effort, until she leaned back in her padded chair.

"Why isn't the TV on?"

Rae went channel by channel until her mother yelled at the opening credits of *Explosión de Amor*.

"You don't even speak Spanish, Mom," Rae argued, forking a large bite of macaroni and cheese. She had filled her plate with it.

"Look in Estela's eyes, you can't see that she's hurting?" Her mother gestured to the thirty-two-inch set. "Did you put cayenne in this? You always make food too spicy." She screwed up her face at her plate.

"The kitchen wench will fix that next time," Rae said.

"Don't use that word in my house," her mother said.

"*Wench* is a bad word?" she asked.

"It's not a good word. I hope you don't use that kind of vocabulary at your job," she said. She looked over to the unused dining room. "That plant needs watering."

"How old were you when you had me?" Rae asked. "Thirty-eight?"

Her mother waved a hand at her. "What did Raúl just say?"

Rae took her plate into the kitchen. She rinsed away remnants of cheese. Before she moved back in, when their relationship had tilted toward friendship, Rae would have told her mother about the appointment. She would have asked her mother if she thought she could still be a mother. She would have called her mother an "old lady" and her mother would have laughed and swatted at Rae's hand. Eighty and wheelchair-bound, Rae's mother didn't get the joke anymore.

"Not Carlos. Goodness! Estela doesn't know what she's doing with her life."

Estela wasn't alone.

After *Explosión de Amor* and after Rae had scrubbed the last dish, she helped her mother to the portable potty by her bed. Some days, it seemed Rae was only tending to her mother's body, feeding it, waiting for her to evacuate it, so Rae could watch her clean it.

"Your father spoke a little Spanish," her mother said.

"I never heard him," Rae said. Twenty years removed from his body, his smell, his voice, Rae sometimes couldn't reconstruct him at all.

"It was just a very little. When we went to Mexico for our honeymoon, it was a big deal, you know. Most black folks didn't do all that, especially none like us who really didn't have money anyway."

"Cancún."

"Yes, but when we got there they didn't have our room. That's what they said, but they didn't want black people in their hotel. Just like here. So your father went around to all the nicest hotels in the city asking, '¿Por favor, un espacio para mi amor?' A space for my love. *Space* was easier for him to pronounce than *room*."

A honeymoon sounded like a quaint oddity, like a corset, a dowry, or getting married at twenty-one.

"How old were you when you started menopause?"

"What did we have for dinner last night?" Her mother's face was puzzled.

"What?" Rae searched her eyes for signs of dementia.

"I don't know the answer to that question either," her mother said. She smacked Rae on her leg.

Rae turned her nose away. It was beginning to smell.

"Don't act like we didn't talk when I was on the toilet even without this bum hip."

"I didn't like it then either, Mom."

"It's called intimacy, Rae. You need more of it in your life," her mother said. She wadded up some toilet paper.

***

Now, Rae and Marcus shared a shredder.

"It's like we have a kid together. Responsibility," Marcus told Rae when she walked in Monday morning to find the square, squat machine on their cubicle wall.

"This is like the responsibility of a plant. Unless you're planning to take the shredder home to make it go night-night."

"Okay, a plant," Marcus agreed. "But it's ours."

They only sat next to each other because the copywriting department had one too few desks. He was in Group/Corporate Furniture Sales. Hotels loved to furnish their lobbies with pieces from Windows and Walls. Marcus said the plushness of the down cushions made excellent perches for high-class hookers.

"Escorts," Rae chastised him.

There wasn't a thing wrong with him. She just wasn't interested in the pudgy contents of Marcus's shirt, until that day she peed on herself. She hadn't planned to mark any territory, but her body had made the decision for her: peeing around Marcus, if not peeing on him.

So, there was the shredder, and before there were the greetings: "Hey, neighbor."

The CEO of Windows and Walls emailed the entire company on Monday mornings and opened each message of corporate encouragement with "Hey, neighbor." But Rae and many of her coworkers found him creepy, his hands too small and white for his buff, orange body. Marcus started saying "Hey, neighbor" in mocking voices. First, a classic: the vampire. Followed by a mob voice and then a blaxploitation voice. That morning, his "Hey, neighbor" eschewed comedy and what was left was more bass than Rae knew from Marcus. It must be his 1970s soul-singer version.

She was drawing a blank on copy for the kids section

of the catalog. Actually not a blank, she was drawing lines and stick figures on the specs for the cribs. Behind a Brazilian timber and a nontoxic plastic choice, she drew two sticks of dynamite and KABOOM in capital, block letters. The stick figure machine-gunned the oak changing tables, but the gun came out all wrong. The slogans weren't going any better. "Put your kid in it" didn't have panache.

She typed "Hey, neighbor" and then deleted it.

On her desk was her lunch, the last orange in the fruit and vegetable bin. She couldn't peel it. She once had scratched her mother helping her off the pot, the flesh of her arm too thin to tolerate Rae's squared-off gel manicure. Her nails were short now and inept at things like peeling fruit.

A screeching noise came out of the shredder.

"We hide too much from people."

Rae turned around. Marcus had a hand on her cubicle wall but stared down at the small metal machine that joined them.

"Why do we need a shredder anyway?" he asked.

"Because there are identity thieves."

"Who pretends to be the furniture described in your catalog copy?"

"For the environment?"

Marcus moved away from the shredder and stepped into Rae's cube. "Maybe. I'll need you to get back to me about that."

"I didn't know I worked for you now."

"I'm sales. You write copy to get people to buy. You clearly work for me."

Rae hadn't known he possessed wit. She picked up her orange, forcing a too-short nail into its skin, in case the admiration showed on her face.

"I thought sales were down."

"Not because of me. Maybe it's the catalog."

"Oh, I'm the failure?"

"I'm suggesting that yes, you might be the sole source of the company's bad fourth quarter."

Rae dropped the orange back on the desk, defeated. "I *am* powerful. Don't you see my lavish surroundings?"

Marcus smiled and picked up the orange. He began to peel it. He talked about the sales reports, the numbers that were down, the numbers that would be up by the end of the month if only the catalog would pull its weight. All the while, he peeled. He didn't do it clean, in one long strip. He did it in shabby starts, orange bits making it mostly to her desk but sometimes landing on the floor. When the peel was gone, he worked on the pith, finding tiny entryways into the cream-and-orange-flecked shroud. This he got off in one strong pull and the covering remained in his hand after he gave the orange back to Rae and said, "But maybe I'm wrong about you."

"You might be," she said, holding the sticky wetness of the fruit in her hands. The smell filled her cubicle and later, at home, she knifed into the peel of an orange to smell it there too. "You might be," she said, turning away from him to place the orange, lightly, gently, onto a nearby paper towel. His hands were chalky, too dirtied to touch anything, but she wanted to reach out.

"I'm gonna get a cookie from that place across the

street. You want one?" he asked. He rubbed his hands together, but the orange only spread, the smell of it only grew.

She shook her head and pointed to the orange. He nodded and took the two steps out of her cubicle. She turned back to her computer screen.

"Hey, neighbor," she heard from behind her and this time she didn't dismiss the bass of the greeting.

* * *

Rae slept in her ex-boyfriends' T-shirts. The collection started with the "Run Joe" T-shirt of her high school boyfriend. She hadn't worn that one in years. Of late, she wore Homeland Security's Marine Corps Marathon 2005 shirt. It had long sleeves, but she cut them off one night, sitting on the floor of his Columbia Heights apartment listening to him snore. She moved the scissors through the thick cotton, making her lines as even as she could. It should look like it had always been that way, as though everything, even cut sleeves, was meant to be.

She pulled Homeland Security's T-shirt off, undoing the silk scarf covering her hair in the process. She laid the cotton under her hips and widened her legs. When she sat up on her elbows, she could still see 2005 in the triangle created by her thighs. Homeland liked that she never wore panties to bed. She was, he said, a woman who knew what she wanted.

From the drawer of her bedside table, she took out

her vibrator, the new one she'd purchased just after the breakup. She waited for her mind to fill with explicit pictures, more of the last lover than the seventeen or so before.

"I'm very competitive," Homeland said. She pictured her vagina as a dartboard. Homeland thought he always hit the bull's-eye, but he was often just a bit out of the winner's circle.

"However rough you give it," he told her one night, her legs in a Romanian-gymnast-back-in-the-day scissor kick, "I'll give it right back."

His giving was always bedroom entrenched. His heart never caught up to his dick. The emotional memories did her no good now. When they were together, thinking of him at his most tender had always helped. Dirty—the talk, the hair pulling, the different positions—got her in the mood. Love helped her stay there.

Now, remembering the cut of his body would make an orgasm possible. She didn't bother with the lower, slower settings on the vibrator. She slid the remote to the highest setting, but the buzz she knew so well did not begin. She flicked the remote off and back on. She tried a lower setting. Still, the vibrator lay next to her, impotent. She didn't want to use her fingers and touch the treacherous female body parts. She pulled Homeland Security's T-shirt back on and tried to go to sleep, but couldn't. Somewhere in the vast walk-in closet in her mother's old bedroom there must be batteries.

The closet was huge and always Rae's favorite place for make-believe. Rae pulled boxes down, stuffed with old receipts, grocery lists, and notebooks in her father's handwriting. Detritus wasn't a life. She found two large garbage bags in the bathroom and wedged all that would fit from the shelves into them. In her grabbing, a package of the newly purchased adult diapers fell, hitting her shoulder on the way to the floor.

For babies, it was freedom to have someone care for you, tend to every cry. People cooed at a child running around in only a diaper. Parents used words like *wee wee* to make bodily functions innocuous and fun. *Incontinence*, *bedpan*, and *catheter*, had no cute rhyming alternatives. She tore into the soft packaging, through to the plastic panties. The closet was dark, but the moon through the large bedroom windows spotlighted the diaper.

She knotted Homeland Security's T-shirt at her belly. The leg openings tugged, a size small meant for her mother's ever-thinning legs. Those spindles set in a bathtub, lowered into a chair, and laid out on too-soft cotton sheets. In the diaper, Rae's legs were even fuller, thicker. The elastic would rub if she had to wear these all day, a greater inconvenience than pads. For days when she wasn't on her period, she could forget her body. Without any period, she would think of her body all the time. An old maid now. An old lady soon enough.

***

Rae didn't remember saying yes to a date with Marcus. She had delivered a tiny smile and a raise of her shoulder. He wanted to go on a weeknight, right after work.

She asked if they could go on a Sunday night instead. She didn't want to be seen leaving the office with him.

Rae asked the home health aide to stay late for overtime pay.

"Is this a date?" her mother asked, waiting at the foot of the stairs in her padded chair.

"He's just someone from work," Rae said. She paused to examine her makeup in a nearby mirror.

"I was thirty-eight when I had you. You're already forty-one."

"This is the conversation I was trying to have the other night."

"Well, just remember that tonight."

"I'll try not to." Rae kissed the top of her mother's head and left.

She parked just a block from the Mexican restaurant on Eighteenth Street. She had been there on dates with Homeland Security and with guys before him. The choice lacked imagination. She pulled into the parking space ten minutes before they were to meet, but she didn't go into the restaurant until ten minutes after. He sat on a bench by the front and rose as she walked in. She didn't apologize for being late.

At the table, he lowered a bright red holiday gift bag onto the table.

"For you," he said.

She plunged her hand into red tissue paper to retrieve a small object. Placed in front of her, she rifled through the contents of her brain to identify it as a statue, a toy, or an exorcism tool.

"It's Baby Jesus," Marcus said.

Rae's rifling stopped on Baby Jesus. He was indeed wrapped in swaddling cloths and laying in, well not a manger, but definitely a made-in-China hard plastic bassinet.

"And look," Marcus said. He pointed to the side of the baby. "This is the gold, frankincense, and myrrh. And when you touch each one . . ." He waited and touched the gold. "Silver and Gold" began playing. Pretty secular, but then heathens bought Christmas decorations too. Baby Jesus moved his animatronic head from side to side, swaying to the tune. Crying must have been beneath the Lord and Savior. "And then," Marcus continued, touching now the frankincense. This time, Rae could pick out "We Three Kings of Orient Are" from the stilted electronic music playing. At the last touch of Marcus, unrepressed in his grinning, the Baby Jesus slowed his sway to a stop and blinked blue eyes closed. "What Child Is This?" began to play.

Rae had never understood the title of the song. It sounded menacing, like the tune Roman soldiers would have injected steroids to before they bust up in people's houses to kill Jewish babies. "What child is this?" she could imagine the one most 'roided up asking. Maybe the same dude who had taken a sword samurai-style to John the Baptist's head. "What child is this?" he'd start the chant off for the rest. "Our child," they'd respond. All this growing louder and louder in the Roman locker room or wherever they changed into their breastplates.

But now, "What Child Is This?" played in the plaintive

one-note tone of a kid's piano instead of the smooth jazziness of the others, she thought less of a big massacre and more of Mary, the virgin with it all. The kid. The omnipresent and generous birth father. The deeply forgiving fiancé. Even the rustically elegant manger. She imagined Mary touching her stomach wondering, *What child is this? What is this in store for me?* Maybe it was true what her mother had told her: stay a virgin. They had all the luck.

"Kind of funny, right?" Marcus asked. He crunched into a salted tortilla chip.

"Yeah, kind of funny," she said. She returned a smile to Marcus, a pittance for his effort.

She played the song again and this time no Romans came to her or even blessed virgins. All she could hear were the opening words: *What child.* What child?

The waitress came to take their order. Rae asked for a pitcher of margaritas even though Marcus said he wanted only one glass. They knew little about each other beyond office-supply preference. He hadn't grown up in DC. She had. He had three siblings. She had none. He asked all the questions and she gave the shortest of answers. The food came and they ate between halting conversation.

"So, what's the best thing about your life?" Marcus asked.

Rae remembered that first dates were interviews for jobs you weren't even sure you wanted. Sometimes, ones for which you hadn't even applied. "The best thing?"

"Or the worst," he said. He laughed after as if his life was free of worst.

"Well, there's copywriting."

"But that can't be the best thing in your life. I mean it's only copywriting."

"It's only sales that you do," Rae said. She pushed her plate away.

"I know," he said. "That's why it isn't the best thing in my life." He was quiet.

"What is then?" Rae asked. She was prepared to hear something inane like his comic-book collection or stupid signed sports memorabilia.

"My record collection," he said. A collection of some sort, she knew it.

"It's only records," she said.

"No, it's my history. It's what my dad collected. I took them all after the funeral," he said. Rae hid her shame by drinking the last of her margarita.

"Writing," she finally said.

"Furniture catalog writing?"

"I used to do other writing."

"What made you stop?" he asked.

Rae waved a hand to dispel his words. "I missed my life. That's all."

"Missed it?" he asked.

"Some nights I should have gone out instead of staying in or stayed in when I went out. And there it would have been: my reason for living. Glowing out of the television screen or something and it would have made all the sense in the world."

"What would have?"

"What I was meant to be," she said. "Or maybe it's better I didn't find out. If the world needs bus drivers and

199

ditch diggers, maybe it also needs unmarried daughters who take care of their mothers and never realize their potential."

"You act like it's all over," he said.

"Maybe it is," she said. She felt loss somewhere in her stomach.

His fingers reached for hers. "You're beautiful," Marcus said.

She was all body, for her mother, for men, for herself. She moved her fingers away from his.

"I was thinking about dessert, but I think it would be better to go without," Rae said.

Marcus placed his napkin on the table. "Then I'll pay and we can go."

When he walked her to her car, he didn't try to kiss her. Through her wool coat she could hardly feel his hands on her back, but when he hugged her, she settled into his chest. She preferred it to Homeland's, no wall of muscle. No well-armed defense.

"I'd like to know you," he whispered into her ear.

Rae had learned early on how to stop the advances of men, it was a skill a girl needed past the age of twelve. She couldn't remember, however—standing in Marcus's arms, his touch light and not lecherous—how to stop the eager fingers of intimacy.

***

She drove home in quiet, but she opened the door to her mother yelling: "Somebody help Estela out!" Rae had missed all of that night's show, but her mother tried to catch her up, sitting in her metal chair positioned in the center of the old claw-foot tub.

Her mother hadn't taken a real bath in decades, the ache of her knees and the twinge of arthritis before she even broke the hip. Rae tried in the beginning to leave her in there by herself, but her mother would stop her with, "I might need you." Now, Rae always stayed. She had tried to get her mother to shower with the home health aide, but she didn't like for the woman to see her privates.

"She already does when she helps you onto the pot," Rae reminded her mother.

"I tell her to look the other way."

Her mother showered at night then, so that Rae could see her privates instead. She liked to announce the washing of them ("Can't forget the queen!") before the cloth descended to the gray, nearly hairless triangle.

Rae wondered if her mother had had sex since her father died. While she was making terrible choices in men, her mother might have been finding a companion, not worried about pregnancy or marriage or how committed he could be. She could worry about her own happiness. And, of course, the queen V. If Rae gave into that vision for her own life, she would have no one to watch her as she washed herself. No child rife with resentment and love would hold out a towel for her and swaddle her as she had once swaddled them.

"How was the date?"

"Fine, Mom," Rae said. She took off her earrings and unbuttoned her blouse.

"You want so much that you end up getting nothing."

"I should just settle for something?" Rae asked. She had witnessed unhappy marriages, women collapsing under the weight of sorrow. If that were going to happen to Rae, then she would do it under the weight of self-imposed sorrow, not sorrow from a husband or from the inescapable clamp of motherhood. Women jumped into the vastness for the meaning a child could bring and found their bodies battered on the way down. She didn't know the possible joy of motherhood, but she did know the search for joy was a crap homework assignment.

"You don't need everything from him. You keep wanting to find everything. Your father just asked for a space on our honeymoon, Rae."

"Mom. You don't understand. You were in your twenties."

"Look how small this bathroom is. But here you are watching me wash myself and that's love. Right here is a space."

Her mother rose from her chair, looming larger than Rae had seen in years. Rae stood and opened out a towel for her mother to step into and hugged her body with its cotton.

That night, Rae didn't put on an ex-boyfriend's T-shirt or slip out of panties to sleep naked. She pulled back her sheets and lay down, fully clothed.

$\star\star\star$

On the front of the catalog was a man walking toward a woman sitting in a Windows and Walls living room. Rae had to copyedit the bulky set of pages before it went to Maggie and then a proofreader. She had come up with a tagline for the opening pages: Furniture You Love for the Room You Love. Rae crossed out *Room* and put *Space*. It was nearly five and she would take the catalog home to edit it over the weekend. There was an *Explosión de Amor* marathon. Her mother had canceled all of Rae's plans.

Marcus hadn't spoken to her all day and Rae figured, although it would make for uncomfortable shredding, it was best.

She packed her bag and began to shut down her computer when she heard a "Hey" behind her.

"I was thinking about getting dinner after work," Marcus said. He looked down at the shredder. "You want to come?"

Rae could think of many reasons to say no, but she found a couple to say maybe and turned those into a yes. They walked to the parking lot and Maggie told them to have a good weekend as they went.

"I could drive us there and drive you back to your car." He argued that it would be easier parking that way. Rae liked that he lied to her.

Rae went to her car and laid the stack of pages for the new catalog on her back seat. In one of the footwells was the package of baby diapers. The brown baby gurgled. She locked the car and checked her hair and makeup in the window.

Once, she was so sure of invincibility: the firmness of her thighs, the elasticity of her heart, the expansiveness of the world whenever she decided to open her arms wide enough to capture the entire thing. And now? She walked toward Marcus, his tie too tight, his car too old, but his smile nicely warm and intimate.

Now, twenty years later, this.

YOU CAN LEAVE,
BUT IT'S GOING TO COST YOU

"Marvin Gaye was a rapper." That's what my father tells me after I've buckled my seatbelt. It's not the first time he has told me something in the hopes that I won't believe him and he'll have to explain. He is an educator without a formal classroom. His lectures are not standard academics. He doesn't bother with a syllabus and a reading list or vocabulary that will impress his students. Instead, when my father gets excited about something, he begins every sentence with *see*.

"See Marvin Gaye was ahead of his time."

"See no one was ready for what he was trying to bring."

"See those knucklehead rappers you listen to, they didn't start that."

"But what year was the album, Daddy? Marvin wasn't cribbing from them?" I ask. My father shakes his head and slams a hand on the dashboard. He can't let some know-it-all thirtysomething kid question his expertise.

"Marvin did not crib from anybody."

WHUR is playing a tribute to Marvin tonight. "Sounds

like Washington" is their tagline. It has been since I was a kid, when I would lie down on the plastic of our old car's back seat and fall asleep to the voice coming out of the speakers and to my parents saying things I couldn't make out. The radio announcer tells us it's the anniversary of Marvin's death. My father claims he already knew this. He lowers his window so he can smoke.

My father likes unfiltered cigarettes. They are killing him, but when he lights up and his eyes flutter closed on the inhalation, I get as much pleasure from it as he does. I never tell him that. He should quit, but won't. He was a big man only in my childhood imagination and now that he has gotten shorter and his upper body has thinned, the cigarettes preserve his manhood. Women used to re-apply lipstick in the presence of his thin, sharp features, but now those features are too fine for the skin they are in, so it sags off his jaw and his cheekbones.

Even though my legs don't need it, I move my seat back so I can see him better. He is still handsome.

Our nights usually start like this. He wants to take a ride so he gets in his car and ends up driving by for me. If I'm not home, he says the drive from Northeast to Shaw is still worth it because he takes it slow and watches all the young people in the neighborhood clogging the narrow sidewalks of U Street. I tell him to call so he'll be sure I'm there, but he likes the surprise. "You never know what is waiting for you," he tells me.

"People use the word *genius* too much," he says.

"You think so?" I ask, manufacturing surprise for his benefit. He's given me this lecture before, but I like to play the attentive student. He pulls on his cigarette, nodding as he does because both the nicotine and the thought are that good.

"Is there genius anymore?" he asks. I don't answer because that's not the way the script goes. I am here only for encouragement, not for debate or dialogue.

"That's a good question."

"No, absolutely not," he says. "Except, Marvin." He turns the radio's volume up. "A Washingtonian," my father says.

I nod. For him, this means I can do anything because like Marvin Gaye I was raised in Washington. Daddy would say it sometimes after one of my failures, like the trumpet lessons that ended in an off-key recital. Or the high school art show where my watercolors stayed two-dimensional when other students' work grew hands to reach out and hold you. "Art is hard," he'd said, considering my watered-down painting. "Look at Marvin Gaye. He was a Washingtonian."

Marvin Gaye gave me permission, my father believed, to be great. It was like how knowing someone who went to college made it more possible for you to go. You knew someone who was already living your dream.

"You can't listen to this like you do your hip hop. It doesn't work when you do that. This, you have to listen to like you care about it. Like someone you love is talking to you and you're trying to hear it all. Hip hop is like somebody yelling at you when you walk down the street." He motions out at Fourteenth Street, packed with people out for some nighttime fun. Parts of Fourteenth Street used to be women and men out for a different kind of nighttime fun, but the sex workers have been spirited away to other blocks. The grit that used to be on these streets has been swept away by overpriced restaurants and residents who think more than two years of living in Shaw makes them the rightful bearers of its legacy. We pass a car thumping with the bass of a hip hop song. I'm too old to know the song. After I hit thirty, music on the radio became a language in which I was no longer fluent. Daddy lost his ear for new music even longer ago. "See? I don't know why you would pay much attention to them anyway. They're yelling at you. This, Marvin, is somebody telling you something important, something real personal that they can't even believe they're about to tell you. So, if you don't listen, get quiet, look them in the eye, and let them know you want to hear what they have to say? They might stop talking. And, Pea, that's the last thing you want to happen."

I'm grown, but he still calls me a child's nickname. Pea, Sweet Pea. Sweet Pea Pie is one of his favorites. It doesn't make any sense, but it does make me smile. Mom said that I would go to school telling them my name was Pea and would never answer when the teacher called for Theresa.

"The problem is people don't want to feel anymore," he says. He bangs on the steering wheel. Wrap-up of lecture number one.

"What's wrong with a good time?" I say. "That's all they want." Sparkling collections of women wobble and strut toward equally bright businesses. The satisfaction of dress-up, of make-believe. Better to be weighed down by too many cocktails than too many worries about where your life is going.

"Not you though," he says. "You've been home more lately?" He asks, but he could have just said it. He is trying to interview when he knows he only wants to analyze.

"That's what old married ladies do."

He laughs, his first of the night. Joy sweeps over his face and clambers down to his chest. He rocks with amusement.

"Hardly old, Pea." His hand goes to his chin, and I think maybe he's feeling his face and considering when old does get you.

"I like staying in." I spend nights on my couch, alone more often than not. Christian is the one who stays out these days, stays away.

"Nothing wrong with that, nothing wrong with that," he says. So, something is wrong with that. When he disagrees, but doesn't feel comfortable saying that he disagrees, he endorses twice. He really doesn't believe it if he says it three times. "No, nothing wrong with that."

"I was going out. A lot," I say. I shift in my seat, the belt feels too tight on my chest. I put it behind me.

"I know," he says. He takes a drag. "That's why I'm wondering why all that before and nothing now."

"Are you worried?" I ask. He makes a left on Rhode Island Avenue. We veer right at Logan Circle. Friends in college who weren't from DC said the street layout was confusing, the roundabouts, state names, alphabet, and numbers an unnecessary maze. When I was learning to drive, I would steer through a roundabout two and three times before I got the exit for the street right. "Now, Pea, this one," Daddy would tell me then.

"Nobody's worried."

"Nobody but you."

"Your mother would be worried."

"About me staying in?" I ask. I breathe out a short laugh. My mother never went out in college, almost never when she and Daddy were first married. They would have people over, smoking people, drinking people, loud-laughing people, dancing-to-Marvin-Gaye people, once or twice a month.

"The question isn't about the staying in, it's about whether life is good," he says, knowing this will quiet me.

"No fair using her lines," I say.

"That's not an answer," he says.

In pictures of my parents when they were young, they always had cigarettes in their mouths or between their fingers and they were always dressed to 1970s perfection. She liked to ask if life was good, and then, because most people would answer yes without even thinking about it, she'd ask, "How good?" It was her way into what you were really feeling. She was an impatient woman who ate before grace, who waited at the door ten minutes before you were supposed to leave. She died of breast cancer two years ago. When she was still going through chemo, my mother asked if Daddy and I knew how the end would go. "I don't have time for your Dad to start crying." "Life good?" she'd ask. "I don't have time for you to tell me what you think I want to hear. If it's good, tell me how good."

He turns into LeDroit Park, hidden behind the showiness of Georgia and Florida Avenues. Everything is new on those streets, but LeDroit is still old. Some of the houses are large, whole corner lots with balconies and porches. Others are smaller row houses crammed onto the block, yards just big enough for a parent and child to fall into a raked pile of leaves. The houses' colorful paint jobs—bright oranges, deep blues, pastel greens—have to do all the elbowing for attention.

"Your mother and I wanted to live in this neighborhood," he says. He snakes his head, neck, and shoulders out the window to look at the turrets atop one of the houses. "White-only until black Washingtonians said, 'Oh no you don't.' You know the greatness that lived in these homes don't you?"

I nod. Judges, doctors, writers, thinkers. He should run tours of historic black Washington. "And to your left, the city that was the crown jewel of black America."

"Washington is filled with elegance," he says. He drives out of LeDroit to Georgia Avenue.

Like me, he is a born and raised Washingtonian, but not her. She grew up in Richmond, but always wanted to live further North. DC was as far as she got because she met my father.

"He only cares about sex," I say, pointing to the radio. A woman is moaning in the background of the song that's on. "You shouldn't listen to this filth, Daddy." I wag a finger at him, taking extra-long sweeps to get him to laugh.

"He's talking about making love, Pea. Physically. Emotionally. Spiritually. The depth on this brother."

It's the first day of April and earlier I could feel the warm air under the cold. The weather is taking its layers off. The cherry blossoms will bloom soon. Christian loves them. We've driven so far down Georgia, it's turned into Seventh Street. We hit Pennsylvania. At night here, the floodlights planted in the grass in front of all the government buildings reflect off the marble. The buildings are like ladies in wedding dresses, their skirts arranged.

"It isn't as quiet Downtown as it used to be," he says. "People hang out down here."

"More money for the city," I say.

"But the quiet I used to like is gone."

"Not by the monuments. Down near the Smithsonian."

"Yeah. Sometimes you need that, a whole world of quiet," he says.

A track I've never heard before comes on. "Did he say, 'Why do I have to pay attorney fees'?"

My father laughs, and I join in, so captivated by the shake of his cheeks. "*Here, My Dear*. He had to pay to get out of his marriage. He paid with the album."

"Marriage," I say. "Maybe I should write a whole album about marriage."

"Could you do it?" he asks.

"The first half at least."

"Why isn't Christian with you when I come by to see

you?" he asks. This must be the reason for tonight's ride.

"The path to true love never did run straight," I say. It is a line from his series of Love talks, one of six.

"What happened?"

"It might be more than you want to hear, Daddy," I say. He used to say that his friends told him having a daughter would change him. "Did it?" I asked as a girl. "Yes," he said. It was one of the first times my father hadn't mused on his answer, said something like, "That question doesn't even begin to get to the answer." Mom had been out of town, visiting family, when he determined that I needed a bra. We went into Woodie's to find one. He pointed me to the lingerie section and told me to tell the saleswoman that my father thought I needed some garments to help me become a woman.

"Come on."

"We're just far apart right now."

"Why?" He takes a left turn up Sixth.

I have always cared more about whether my father was proud of me. My mother's pride in me felt unmovable, a boulder anchoring everything else in my life. His love I never questioned, that he would do for me, provide for me. I wasn't sure if he only thought I *could* be great or if he thought I *was* great just as I was, without artwork, with my accounting degree, with my desk job.

"I cheated on him." We're at a light in front of the synagogue on Sixth and I, and that's about right, I could go get some forgiveness. Maybe they'll let a girl raised praising Jesus in there just this once if she's desperate enough.

Daddy starts to nod as if I've told him this story before. He nods as if he knew just the way he knew this was the anniversary of Marvin's death. We ride up Sixth in silence. I shouldn't have told him. He'll tell me how wrong I am. Love is a garden, this is another saying he uses. I have not tended my garden.

The Marvin song playing is a cappella at the end, and it gets even quieter in the car. He rolls the window up and then says, "I cheated on your mother," like someone outside might hear him. I expect to lose my breath, but I don't. It makes me feel better to know I'm not alone and that feels terrible.

"When?" I ask because it may be the only question that actually matters anymore.

"A long time ago," he says.

If he'd said he did it when she was sick and dying, I don't know if I would have gotten out of the car. I'm not sure people do that in real life, fling themselves out of moving vehicles. They might only do it in the movies, but I understand the propulsion that anger can give you. I would have needed to get it out.

"When I was in high school?" I ask. He turns his head to me so fast, I know that even if he denies it, I'm right.

"Why you think then?" he asks. He lights a new cigarette, rolls his window back down. He rides by the reservoir across from Howard, the moon filtering into the water this time of night. The clock tower on campus is lit. Daddy could visit me during the day, but he never does. Some things you can say only when the streetlights are on and only parts of the world are illuminated.

"You all were different." I couldn't remember anything specific, no big blowups. They were both more given to explosive laughter than explosive anger, but every room in that house where they were together felt tilted on its side.

"I told her and she'd been waiting on it," he says.

"She knew?"

"Everything. Always."

"That's true." In high school, I started smoking, long drags on unfiltereds just like him. She stopped me in the kitchen one day and brought her face to mine. She closed her eyes and sniffed. She pulled me into her and said, "Why do you smell like him?"

He takes Columbia Road over, but doesn't keep going toward Columbia Heights. He makes a left down Thirteenth Street back toward Shaw and my empty home. We ride and ride and then the car crests the hill at Clifton. All of Washington is laid out before us. The Monument lit. The Capitol close enough to pick up and pocket.

"I thought we might not make it. I thought about leaving."

"Why didn't you?" I ask. Maybe it's something I can tell Christian.

He shrugs and puffs on the cigarette. "I would think, *Today I'm gonna move out*, and then I wouldn't. That happened a few more days. Until, one of those days I realized I wanted to stay."

He pulls up in front of my condominium. A man is walking from down the block, but it's too shadowy to see his face. He walks slowly, his back is so straight, rigid. When he gets to the front door, I see that it's Christian.

"He was sacred, Marvin was," my father says. "But then you know too, he was this blasphemy. How can you not love that?"

He turns the flashers on and turns the music down a bit. The car makes a soft click every time the lights blink. Over them, Marvin tells his ex-wife, tells me and Daddy, "May you always think of me the way I was."

He reaches out for my hand, the darkness making it hard for him to find. We sit like that for a while and listen.

ACKNOWLEDGMENTS

My deepest gratitude to everyone at the Feminist Press, especially my editorial team: Jamia Wilson, whose kindness and creativity during this process were invaluable; Lauren Rosemary Hook, who was one of the first champions of my book; Tess Rankin, whose careful and sensitive copyediting helped make the book better; and Alyea Canada for her conscientious proofreading. Thank you to Suki Boynton for her beautiful cover design, to Jisu Kim for her attentive and dynamic marketing of the book, and to Jennifer Baumgardner, Tayari Jones, Melissa Sipin, and Ana Castillo for believing in the book. I am also grateful to those organizations who have supported my work over the years and enabled this book to be written: Voices of Our Nations Arts Foundation, Hurston/Wright Writers Workshop, Callaloo Creative Writing Workshop, Norman Mailer Writers Colony, and Millay Colony for the Arts; and to the writing teachers and mentors from those workshops, in particular, Mat Johnson and Jeffery Renard Allen.

Thank you to my teachers at New Mexico State University: Rus Bradburd, Robert Boswell, Lily Hoang, Craig Holden, Connie Voisine, Peter Fine, and Joyce Garay. And also to all of my workshop colleagues, but especially: Josh Bowen, Melanie Sweeney Bowen, Phil Hurst, Anna Pattison, and Chris Schacht, who were my first readers.

To my Chicago writing group: LaTanya Lane, Nura Maznavi, CP Chang, and Cole Lavalais. Our workshops made these stories better and challenged me to keep at it even when I wanted to give up. You were all vital to my finally feeling at home in Chicago.

Many thanks also to the community of writers and creative people I've assembled over the years who have been mentors or colleagues, but most of all friends: Bridgett M. Davis, Eisa Ulen Richardson, Marissa Johnson-Valenzuela, Nicole Lawrence, Sarah Herrington, Lisa Ko, Sarah Robbins, Audrey Petty, Lolly Bowean, and Natalie Y. Moore.

Thank you to my family, the Ackers, the McGills, the Latimers, the Bashams, and the Allens, as well as the entire extended Livingston clan.

To my parents, Daniel and Fay Acker: your love of books, conversation, and black folks helped make me a writer.

In particular to my mother, Fay Acker: Your comfort, intellectual curiosity, and faith are boundless. I hope I've made the little girl who read books in the space between the wall and the radiator very proud.

And to my sister, Juliette Acker: No one could have a better sister or a more loving friend. We have shared both physical and emotional space for our dreams, and this dream would not be coming true without you.

To my many wonderful girlfriends from coast to coast and around the world, this book is for you. Many of these characters exist because of the rhythms of your laughter, the conversations over long boozy brunches, and your heart and dynamism. In particular, thanks to Jina Johnson, Traci Curry, and Stacey Barney for being early and encouraging readers. To Olivia McGill for being the best sister-cousin a girl could have. And to Trinishia Samuels, Turkiya Lowe, Joy Fejokou, Aleisia Gibson, and DeDe Brown for all the years of friendship.

To James Britt, thank you for the love, support, endlessly fascinating conversation, and invaluable partnership.

© James Britt

CAMILLE ACKER holds a BA in English from Howard University and an MFA in Creative Writing from New Mexico State University. Her writing has appeared in *Hazlitt* and *VICE*, among other outlets. Raised in DC, she currently lives in Philadelphia.

More Contemporary Fiction
from the Feminist Press

La Bastarda by Trifonia Melibea Obono,
translated by Lawrence Schimel

Black Wave by Michelle Tea

Give It to Me by Ana Castillo

Go Home! edited by Rowan Hisayo Buchanan

Into the Go-Slow by Bridgett M. Davis

Love War Stories by Ivelisse Rodriguez

Maggie Terry by Sarah Schulman

Pretty Things by Virginie Despentes,
translated by Emma Ramadan

The Restless by Gerty Dambury,
translated by Judith G. Miller

Since I Laid My Burden Down by Brontez Purnell

Though I Get Home by YZ Chin

We Were Witches by Ariel Gore

The Feminist Press is a nonprofit educational organization founded to amplify feminist voices. FP publishes classic and new writing from around the world, creates cutting-edge programs, and elevates silenced and marginalized voices in order to support personal transformation and social justice for all people.

See our complete list of books at
feministpress.org